ONE MAN'S TRASH

RYAN SOUTHWICK

Published by Water Dragon Publishing
waterdragonpublishing.com

An imprint of Paper Angel Press
paperangelpress.com

ISBN 978-1-957146-70-6 (Trade Paperback)

FIRST EDITION

10 9 8 7 6 5 4 3 2 1

To Arfer
The loveliest Cockney to ever grace our lives

ACKNOWLEDGEMENTS

To all the authors who breathed life into the Truck Stop, I hope the legacy long continues.

To Steve, for creating tomes of technical documents that made the Truck Stop station a believable place.

To Niki, for hitting a cover home run on the first try. Keep them coming!

To Dick and Karen, my childhood playmates, mentors, and Cockney correctors.

To Louise, for the amazing beta feedback that you turned around on a moment's notice. You're my reading hero!

And to Arfer, born within the sound of Bow bells, who taught me true Cockney rhyming slang at a young age, along with a host of other life skills that made me the person I am today. You will always be missed.

1

CROFT

CROFTON WINDER FLOATED OUT from the stasis room, rubbed the drug-induced sleep from his eyes, and gazed blearily out the cockpit. He blinked, then rubbed his eyes again to make sure he wasn't still dreaming.

The Truck Stop at the Center of the Galaxy loomed larger than any non-celestial object Croft had ever seen. With the massive accretion disk of the galaxy's core behind it, shimmering every color imaginable, the alien-built space station looked truly majestic. The vastness of space around them glowed with tightly packed stars, swirling, dancing in all dimensions.

Here, the galaxy felt truly alive.

A minute later, Maria emerged from the stasis room. Although she had just awakened, her eyes were already glued to her infernal data pad, which never seemed to leave her hands these days. She scratched her bobbed, dark brown hair, which stuck out in all directions like a giant fuzz ball. She shoved a fist in her mouth to stifle a yawn, as if the most stunning display in the galaxy paled next to whatever business-related page had caught her attention.

Rallying himself, Croft wrapped an arm around her shoulders and smiled.

"What did I tell you? Not bad for a summer getaway, eh?"

Maria reluctantly pried her gaze from her data pad and looked out the cockpit window. Her breath caught.

Croft squeezed her shoulders, the little rabbit in his chest hopping around in glee.

Finally. *Finally* he had found something to engage her other than her business. It had taken a twenty-six-thousand light-year skipstream trip to the center of the galaxy to do it, but the expense — which, on Croft's meager mechanic's income, he would be paying down for years to come — had been worth it.

Maria's attention soon returned to her data pad, dragging Croft's heart down with it. She sat in one of the two forward-facing seats, set her pad on the console and, Croft suspected, forgot all about the marvelous wonder outside their window.

A red light flashed on the control panel. Someone was hailing them on an emergency channel.

Not good.

Croft sat in the pilot's chair and opened the communication channel. "This is Crofton Winder of the *SS Majestic*. What —"

A loud *beep* cut him off. A message had arrived with high importance, embedded with an autopilot program. The subject read:

COLLISION IMMINENT! RUN THE ATTACHED PROGRAM IMMEDIATELY.

Collision?

He glanced through the cockpit window. The space station ahead appeared larger than before.

Much larger.

Croft quickly pulled up the autopilot status.

AUTOPILOT OFFLINE. ERROR CODE: 80043.1

Crap!

One glance at the rapidly looming space station told him they had no time to reboot it. They had exited the skipstream off-target and at a higher-than-projected velocity — punctuated by a belated collision alarm.

Their ship was hurtling straight for the station's Main Ring.

The chances of the autopilot failing were staggeringly low. The chances of also exiting the skipstream on a collision course with another celestial object were so ridiculously small that Croft had a better chance of winning the lottery three times in a row.

In this case, he felt anything but lucky.

Maria's stared at the oncoming catastrophe with wide-eyed shock. Her mouth opened, then snapped shut when Croft pounded the "Load" button with his fist. Whatever nav program the message contained wouldn't be as good as a full autopilot, but it would be better than the non-existent pilot they had now.

A loading screen flashed on the display, followed immediately by a "Run" prompt.

Maria mashed the screen with her thumb.

The ship pitched ninety degrees downward, leaving Croft's stomach a few kilometers behind. Thrusters roared to maximum, plastering both of them against the back of their seats.

The thrusters cut almost as quickly as they'd started. The ship pitched upward again, putting the space station back in view.

They were still hurtling toward it at mind-boggling speed — so fast that Croft couldn't tell whether they would crater into the lower dock ring, or into one of the four long arms connecting the outer ring to the station's cylindrical center.

Alarms blared.

Collision imminent! Collision imminent!

The message flashed repeatedly — and unhelpfully — across the screen.

Maria's data pad clattered to the floor. She dug her fingers into his arm, eyes wide with terror.

"CroooooooOOOOOFFFTTT!!!"

He tensed, pressing himself against the seat, as if that would improve his chances in the slightest of surviving a three-hundred-thousand-kilometer-per-hour collision with the massive space station.

Majestic streaked forward. The station's outer ring grew impossibly large in the blink of an eye.

The ship rocked, as if hit from the top and bottom simultaneously.

And then the station disappeared, leaving only an amazing view of the galaxy's super-massive black hole.

Croft pinched himself to make sure he hadn't died. It hurt almost as much as Maria's fingers, which dug painful divots into his arm.

The collision warning disappeared from the console, replaced with a lateral image of their ship. The top and bottom flashed yellow, citing eighty-one and eighty-eight percent structural integrity, respectively.

Otherwise, *Majestic* appeared to be fine.

Croft turned to Maria. A gigantic smile stretched his cheeks. Maria slowly faced him, trembling. A smile slowly spread across her face, too, reminding him of the day they'd first met, over a year ago. These days, her smiles were too few and far between. Seeing it only reminded him how much he missed the old Maria. That it had taken a near-death experience to make her bloom saddened him, but it also gave him hope.

This wondrous space station, built by the long-extinct Delphians, would make her smile again. It had to.

Another incoming request interrupted his reminiscence — this time, *not* on the emergency channel. A glance showed the same ship ID as the emergency hail.

"Is everyone all right?" a female voice said the moment he opened the comm.

"Yes, thanks to you," Croft said.

"Thank goodness! I wasn't sure if the nav instructions I sent would be compatible with your systems, so I made a best guess." Her light and airy voice reminded Croft of a warm breeze on a pleasant summer day.

Not compatible?

All Earth ships used the same navigation software, or near enough, which meant the person on the other end of the call wasn't human.

And I'll bet she's a station traffic control operator.

"You'll have to let me buy you a drink when we finally dock," Croft said before his brain could filter the suicidal response.

A stern glance from Maria confirmed he'd flown into a galactic minefield.

"U-us, I meant." Croft tugged his collar, which had suddenly grown hot. "Let *us* buy you a drink. Me and Maria. We're a couple."

"Oh," the voice said, so sadly and softly that Croft wanted to reach through the console and give her a comforting pat on the shoulder. "That's nice. The drink will have to wait, unfortunately. I'm here on bus —"

Static momentarily buzzed the console.

"Sorry," the voice said, even softer than before. "I have to go. Glad you're safe, and hope you have a wonderful stay."

"Wait! What's your —"

The comm link died.

"— name."

Croft sat back in his chair. The tone of her voice — Croft could only think of it as a *she* — had changed after the static interruption.

Was she afraid?

"Terrific," Maria said, gripping her hair. "She probably reported us to the local authorities."

"Why would she do that?"

"For damaging the station!"

Maria tapped the console. A view from the outside cameras appeared. She rewound a few minutes back, then set the playback speed to one-one thousandth of normal. Even at that slow speed, they approached the station frighteningly fast, but it soon became clear why they hadn't vaporized against its titanium exterior. The bottom of *Majestic* had scraped the very top of the station's Main Ring. Nanoseconds later, the top of their ship had scraped the bottom of one of the four large spokes connecting the Main Ring to the center of the station.

Croft's jaw dropped.

Their ship had essentially threaded a needle. A centimeter higher or lower and the impact vibrations alone would have torn them apart. Croft doubted even their autopilot, had it been functioning, could have pulled off such a precise maneuver. Whoever their savior was, she had performed a certified miracle.

"This is terrible," Maria said in a hollow voice.

"That we survived?"

"That we're ruined! *I'm* ruined!" She stood and started pacing, waving her hands. "Do you have any idea how much it costs to fix a *space station?* One built by extinct aliens, at that!"

"Maria —"

"Don't 'Maria' me! This is my ship. I'm responsible!" She looked around wildly. Her eyes darted like a trapped animal. "They'll confiscate it. Sue me for reckless flying and endangerment of the station's inhabitants. They … they might arrest me!" Maria grabbed his shoulders and shook until his teeth rattled. "I can't go to jail, Croft! No one will ever do business with me again! I can't!"

"You won't."

She sucked a panicked breath to protest, but Croft pulled her into his lap and held her close. Her body sank against his, stiff and trembling.

"I'll fix this," he whispered into her hair. "You'll see."

Maria's voice turned deadly soft. "Was this your fault?"

"Me?"

"Were you tinkering again? Is that why the autopilot failed?"

Croft tried to stammer a response, but he couldn't even form the words.

The fault *wasn't* his. He would stake his life on it. Croft had run a cursory diagnostic before they'd departed Earth, nothing more.

"Maybe," he said anyway. If shifting the blame to him would calm her down, then he would gladly take the heat. He hated seeing her so upset. So vulnerable. "And when the authorities ask, I'll tell them as much."

Her shaking subsided. Maria rubbed her nose, sniffled, and rotated in the zero gravity until Croft could only see her back.

"Good."

Without another word, she kicked off and floated back to the stasis room, which doubled as a bedroom, then locked the door.

Croft pointed the ship back toward the station and began the long process of reversing their velocity so they could return to the Truck Stop, where he hopefully wouldn't be arrested on sight.

2

BAGGAGE

A BARRAGE OF SCENTS greeted Croft when he and Maria ascended the docking ramp: some pungent, some sweet, some acrid, and some so alien that his nose couldn't quite categorize them. A rounded ceiling loomed thirty meters overhead, more spacious than any space station Croft had ever visited.

And this is just the Docking Ring. The Main Ring is even larger.

Unfortunately, three figures in blue security outfits awaited them at the top of the ladder, each carrying holstered sidearms. Handcuffs dangled from their belts.

Maria stopped in her tracks, rigid. It was exactly as she'd feared.

"Croft," she said so softly that only he could hear. "I ... I can't ..."

He patted her arm to help ease her panic, even though his own heart hammered in his chest like a three-liter piston. Croft had no desire to go to jail, either. But, between the two of them, it wasn't even a choice.

Besides, being in jail is far better than being dead. I'll take what I can get.

Gathering his courage, he motioned for Maria to stay put, then approached the security team.

"Good afternoon," Croft said as affably as he could manage, given the crushing tension in his chest. "Or evening. What time is it here, anyway? Stasis always throws my internal clock for a loop."

Surprisingly, the officers paid him little mind, their attention focused somewhere down the docking ring.

One with a blonde mustache gave him an annoyed look and pulled out his data pad. "Afternoon, if you're on Earth time." He looked away.

"Right, thanks for that Officer ...?"

"Robins."

"Officer Robins. Yes." Croft rubbed his hands. "Well, I can see you're busy, so we'll just, um, head into the station, then, I suppose."

The security team gave no indication that they'd heard or cared. But they hadn't objected, nor had they slapped him in irons, so he considered it a win.

Croft turned and held out his arm. "Shall we?"

Maria squeaked something and hurried up the ramp. Croft was delighted when she accepted his arm, but her tight grip indicated it was probably to keep her upright rather than out of affection.

"Hold up," Robbins said from behind them.

Maria stumbled. Thankfully, Croft caught her before she crashed to the floor. Her entire body trembled, eyes wide with terror. Her breaths came in short, sharp gasps. She was as close to losing it as Croft had ever seen.

He had to fix this.

Croft turned to reply, but it seemed the order hadn't been directed at them. The security team were focused on a pair of scruffy humans who had just emerged from the next ramp over. A couple, Croft guessed from their touching elbows.

Robbins, who appeared to be in charge, stepped forward, hand on his weapon. Thankfully, it stayed in its holster. The couple didn't look nearly as intimidated as Croft thought they should be.

The man's unevenly shaved face twisted into a grin. "Problem, officers?"

"That depends on you, *treasure hunter.*" Robbins spat the last phrase, leaving no doubt about his distaste for the unscrupulous looters who, in most people's opinions, were only a half-step above pirates. "Truck Stop is a Delphian station, but it's Earth-run. All Delphian technology is long gone, just like their civilization over four hundred years ago."

"So sorry to hear that," the woman said, her thickly painted lips turned down in a mock frown. Her upper lip peaked in a V that reminded Croft of a spider. "Good thing we're only here on holiday. Isn't that right, Sturm?"

Sturm nodded, not taking his eyes from the officer. "Too right, Pitts. See? You boys have nothing to worry about."

"It's my job to worry. I suspect everyone, especially those with questionable reputations. Where I get cranky is when I'm right." Robbins closed in until they were nose to nose. "Don't make me right, Sturm. We're a long way from Earth. The only justice here is Mr. Zeno's, and he doesn't take kindly to those who disrespect his property. Got it?"

Pitts purred. She boldly ran a finger down Robbins' cheek. "Officer, we'll be the perfectest little angels you've ever seen. You won't even know we're here."

Robbins looked unconvinced. "You've been warned. Know that Mr. Zeno doesn't give second chances. Have a nice day."

He and the rest of the security team unblocked the corridor. Sturm and Pitts tipped their heads to Robbins on their way by, then flashed grins at Croft and Maria before disappearing down the curved ring corridor.

"Sorry about that."

Croft jumped when he realized Robbins was addressing him.

"Th-that's all right, officer," Maria said, the first to find her voice. She straightened into a business posture that Croft recognized all too well. "We appreciate your diligence. Order is important, especially out here in the middle of nowhere."

"True. Still, I feel guilty that exchange was your first experience aboard the station. Let me send you a few credits to get your vacation back on track. You can cash them in at any establishment." Robbins consulted his data pad. "*SS Majestic?*"

Maria nodded.

"You must be Ms. Gobber, then. Welcome to the Truck Stop at the Center of the Galaxy."

"Thank you."

Another officer cleared his throat. He leaned toward Robbins and showed his own data pad.

"Oh." Robbins regarded them with fresh eyes. "Seems you had a bit of an adventure coming out of skipstream. What happened?"

Maria tensed again. Her fingernails dug painfully into Croft's arm. *Oh boy, here we go.*

"Autopilot failure," Croft said. "Probably my fault. I might have accidentally done, erm, *something* when running the pre-flight diagnostic."

"Autopilot failure during skipstream? Bad luck, friend, but I'm glad you made it in one piece."

"That makes three of us, believe me."

Robbins consulted his data pad. "You're a spaceship mechanic, if I read your profile right?"

"Ten years now. Apprenticed at Jarvey Shipyard, back in the day."

"I know mechanics can be protective sometimes, but do you mind if our engineers have a look at your ship's systems? Incidents like this are practically unheard of. If any outside factors were involved that might create a similar problem for other ships, I'd like to get ahead of the ball."

I guess he was serious about it being his job to worry.

"Of course." Except, mechanic or not, Croft's permission meant nothing because it wasn't his ship. Maria didn't object, however, so it was probably good enough. "We'll send you the access codes."

"Appreciated."

"Likewise. I've got to say, you have a crack crew here. The lady who sent that nav program to us should be given a medal. We'd have been space dust for sure."

"Nav program?" Robbins frowned at the data pad. "I don't see anything in the incident report about us sending a nav program. You sure it was one of our people?"

"Well … no, I suppose not."

"If you find out who she is, buy her a beer from me. She saved me a mountain of paperwork."

Croft chuckled, choosing to believe the omission about he and Maria not dying was an intentional joke.

An awkward silence settled, thicker than old engine lubricant, until Maria cleared her throat.

"So … are you going to press charges?"

"Not unless you intentionally tried to crater yourselves against the station. Did you?"

"N-no, of course not!"

"Then I wouldn't worry."

"Thank you." Maria took a deep breath and straightened the lapels of her business suit. Croft had begged her to wear something less formal, but she'd worn it anyway. "Now, where can we find a meal? And a stiff drink?"

"The Great Mall is probably your best bet. The closest spoke is a hundred meters down that way." Robbins gestured the direction Sturm and Pitts had gone. "Take the elevator up to the Main Ring. Transportation tubes run spinwise and anti-spinwise. If you're looking for a top-notch dining experience, I recommend The Restaurant."

Croft scratched his head. "Sorry, but *which* restaurant?"

"That's its name. Take the spinwise transport tube to the Green Quadrant, which is the next one over, and tell any green android you want to dine at The Restaurant. It will know exactly where to take you. Their Torian stew is amazing." Robbins hoisted his belt. "Anyway, we have to be going. Hope you get a chance to relax while you're here." He started away.

"Hang on!" Croft fished out his wallet and pressed a few bills into his hand. "This is *not* a bribe by any measure, just a thank you."

Curiously, Robbins didn't even balk. He pocketed the money, tipped his head in thanks, and then led his team away.

The floor next to them opened without warning, exposing a hole large enough to swallow three people. From its depths rose a blue-painted robot with far too many appendages. It hobbled forward on two sturdy, rectangular legs, large metal feet clanking across the floor. It extended one of its many thin, metallic arms in greeting.

"Uh, hi," Croft said. He hesitated only briefly before accepting the robot's three-fingered, claw-like hand.

"Greetings!" The robot's mechanical timbre matched its rough and functional construction. "I am Taft. Is your luggage located near the airlock?"

"No, sorry. I was about to gather them up."

"Please allow me, Mr. Winder. If they are equipped with standard Earthen tracking tags, I will have no trouble locating them."

Darn it.

"Actually, no, they aren't." Croft had meant to put tracking tags on them before leaving Earth, but, in the flurry of packing, he'd completely forgotten.

"Oh." Taft's binocular eyes glanced down the ramp, then back at Croft. "Could I trouble you to describe them?"

"Sure, they're ..." Croft frowned, suddenly unable to remember what a single piece of their luggage looked like. "On second thought, it's probably easier if I show you."

Maria fidgeted next to him, shuffling from foot to foot. The confidence on her face had disappeared again, replaced with a worry that he recognized. She was beyond frazzled, and barely holding herself together. For a moment, her eyes smoldered with anger, as if this entire situation really were Croft's fault and he had somehow engineered these series of events to annoy her.

Just like that, her accusatory glare disappeared. Maria swallowed and looked away.

Indecision tore at him. Maria clearly wanted to leave, probably to guzzle that stiff drink she mentioned. But leaving Taft to sort through the luggage Croft had forgotten to tag wasn't fair, either.

He rubbed Maria's shoulders and flashed a warm smile. "Why don't you run ahead to The Restaurant? I'll take care of the luggage and join you in a jiffy."

Maria looked longingly down the ring toward the elevator. "Just a jiffy?"

"As jiffyingly as I can."

"All right." Maria leaned close. For a happy instant, he thought she might kiss him, but she instead whispered in his ear, "Don't forget my suits. They're in the stasis closet next to the EVAs."

"N-no, of course not."

She patted his chest, hesitated as if she wanted to say more, then shook her head and walked in the same direction the security team had gone.

Croft sighed. His romantic vacation plans were off to a terrible start.

Trying not to let despair bring him down, he turned to Taft with a pleasant smile, gestured to the docking ramp, and followed the robot down.

•　　　•　　　•

Once their bags had been rounded up in the middle of the cabin, Taft put his many arms to use and hooked one on each, like a walking coat rack for luggage.

"Thanks, Taft," Croft said.

"My pleasure, Mr. Winder. Your luggage will be in your room within the next eighteen Earthen minutes. Please enjoy your stay." Taft turned to the exit.

"Wait!"

Croft reached for his wallet, but remembered he'd given the last of his loose cash to the security officer. He desperately patted his pants. The little robot couldn't leave without a personal token of appreciation, no matter how small.

A jingle in his back pocket gave Croft an idea. He withdrew a handful of worn coins of various sizes and colors, then sifted through them until he found the perfect one.

"Now," Croft said, "I could just transfer your tip electronically, like everyone else, but before you scoff at this meager coin, please hear me out."

Taft remained quiet. It leaned forward, binocular eyes focused on the proffered coin.

"My dad always believed that tips show true gratitude and respect. As such, a tip should be something precious or meaningful to the service receiver. Electronic transfers are impersonal; I can't touch or feel them, and the bits and bytes that represent them hold no meaning to me. Unlike this coin."

Taft leaned closer. It glanced up at Croft and tilted its head.

Croft rolled the coin across his knuckles with practiced ease, then flipped it into the air. Light danced from its wear-polished faces. He caught it and held it out again.

"Coins are real," Croft said. "Tangible. Each has character and history transcending owners and time."

"What is this one's history?"

"Only the coin could tell us for sure, and they don't talk much. What I can tell you is that this is an ancient currency called a 'quarter.' It predates Earth's discovery of skipstream travel by at least a hundred years. See here …" Croft ran his finger over its practically smooth surface. "If you look closely, you can make out the face of the minting country's first president."

"It is barely visible," Taft said.

"Exactly. This coin has been through so many hands that its features have worn flat. Just so you know, that's a *lot* of hands. Imagine all the things this coin has been used to purchase: bread, bubble gum, cigarettes, a child's toy. Over and over and over. It's been in purses, piggy banks, slot machines, bank vaults, wallets, registers, and pockets."

"Including yours." Taft tore its binocular eyes from the coin and focused on Croft. "Why would you give away such a precious piece of history to a robot you do not know?"

"Because this coin's journey isn't done. Aliens of every species come through the Truck Stop. Coins are no longer accepted as currency, but I can pass it on to someone who appreciates this little gem for what it is. Maybe you'll add to its history, then eventually give it to someone who might take it far, far away, where it can enrich an entirely different culture's history."

Croft pinched it between his fingers and held it out. Taft looked between him and the coin, then hesitantly plucked it from his grasp. A tiny compartment opened beneath one of its arms, where Taft gingerly deposited the coin. The compartment snapped shut. Taft patted it with a satisfied *whir* from somewhere deep in its chest.

"I shall do my best to add to the coin's story."

Without another word, Taft turned toward the exit and disappeared through the airlock.

After one last check, Croft sealed *Majestic,* followed Taft up the ramp, and headed for the elevator. After the long skipstream journey, the centripetal force used to simulate gravity felt like a fifty-pound weight on his back. He paused at the next docking berth to stretch his legs.

From the hole leading down to the airlock, a rough male voice barked something in a language Croft had never heard before. Fortunately, his data pad had, and dutifully translated into English through his earpiece.

"I told you, I'll be back when I'm back. Find something to entertain yourself while I'm gone, but *don't* keep calling me!"

Footsteps ascended the metal ramp. The face that appeared was humanoid, but definitely not human. A thick mane of black, fur-like hair topped his brick-red skin. Violet eyes seemed surprised to find Croft standing there. Croft hadn't realized the creature had been upset until a bold smile broke across his face, exposing sharp, predator teeth.

"Women, eh?" the red alien said a little too easily. His actual words were nothing more than growls and grunts to Croft's untrained ear, but his translator interpreted them almost real-time. "There's no pleasing them."

Croft opened his mouth to object, but found himself nodding. "Why are you with her, then?"

The question surprised even himself; it was inappropriate even among close friends, let alone a complete stranger, and an alien stranger at that.

"I ask myself that same thing."

The red alien stretched. Broad shoulders and thick arms suggested he was many times stronger than Croft. He scratched his cheek with a black, talon-like fingernail, looking thoughtful.

"She didn't start out so needy. Then one day, poof! No matter how much I give her, or how much time I invest, it just isn't enough." He shook his head, sending shimmering waves down his black mane. "Definitely not what I signed up for."

"So what are you going to do? I can't imagine she's happy with the situation, either."

"She isn't. And, truth be told, it isn't her fault. But it ain't mine, either." His toothy grin returned in force. "Look at me! Ain't five minutes docked and I'm already whining to the first person who'll listen." He surprised Croft by sticking his hand out in traditional Earthen greeting. "Name's Kaizon Terazod."

"Crofton Winder," he said, accepting it. Kaizon's crushing grip brought a tear to his eye. "What brings you to the center of the galaxy?"

"Hope," Kaizon said. His smile momentarily faltered, but he shook his head. "I'm a water trader. Heard this old garbage heap of a station might need one."

"Oh?" Croft couldn't keep the disappointment out of his voice. *Is that why Maria came here? To strike a deal?*

If so, Kaizon might well be competition.

Selfishly, Croft couldn't bring himself to care. He hadn't spent his life savings on this trip just so she could bury herself in her business, like she usually did.

"I've heard that's quite a lucrative trade," Croft said carefully.

"It is when you have the right connections, which is exactly what I'm here to build." Kaizon sized him up. "What planet are you from?"

"Earth."

"Ah! The envy of the galaxy when it comes to water. I won't be selling any to you, now, will I?"

"Afraid not."

"Are you a water trader?"

"No, I'm a ship mechanic. But Maria is." Croft bit his tongue at the accidental admission, but it was too late.

Sorry, Maria.

"Maria?"

"Yes, my, um … my girlfriend." At least, Croft hoped she still was.

"Hmm. Is she waiting on your ship while you conduct business?"

As if. "No, she went ahead to The Restaurant. I was just taking care of the luggage and am on my way to join her."

"You let your woman go first? Strange planet, your Earth."

Croft blinked. "Why wouldn't I?"

"Never mind." Kaizon flashed a sharp-toothed grin and wrapped a burly arm around Croft's shoulders. "Tell you what: I hate eating alone, and I don't know anyone on this station. Let me join you two for dinner, and the meal's on me. What do you say?"

Everything Croft knew about the red-skinned alien told him dinner with Maria would be a bad idea. She didn't tolerate chauvinism, and for good reason. Kaizon, on the other hand, was a walking women's rights violation. She would chew him up and spit him out the airlock, assuming he didn't use his sharp teeth to eat her first.

The floor next to them opened, momentarily saving Croft from having to answer. Up rose a multi-limbed robot, similar to Taft, also painted blue, but with different patterns.

"Welcome, Mr. Terazod," the robot said in Kaizon's language. "I am here to collect your —"

"Luggage. Yes, I know, but I assume you can do that *without* interrupting our conversation. Or are you last decade's model?"

The robot took a step backward. Its binocular eyes looked at Kaizon, then Croft, and back again. "I am Liandri Corporation's model A42835 fully autonomous, premium hotel service rob —"

"Egads! Just be quiet and do your job." Kaizon pointed down the airlock ramp. "My ship is *that way.* Luggage is tagged with galaxy-standard locators. Goodbye!" He spun Croft around by the shoulders and started walking them away. "Impossible to find good automated help these days. All they do is yap, yap, yap. Am I right?"

"Oh, actually … That reminds me, I forgot to tell my own luggage bot that one of our bags is fragile." Croft felt guilty lying to his new acquaintance, but he felt even worse for the hard-working robot who had just been so rudely treated. "Why don't you walk ahead? I'll meet you at the elevator."

"All right. Good luck getting through to that pile of scrap." Kaizon patted Croft's back hard enough to knock the wind out of him, then waved over his shoulder and headed off.

The robot started down the ramp, but Croft tugged it to a stop.

"Hang on a sec." He dug in his pocket, fished out the coins, and held one up. "For you."

Unlike Taft, this bot didn't hesitate. It gingerly accepted the coin. "What is this coin's story, Mr. Winder?"

Croft grinned. Apparently, word about Taft's tip had already spread.

"This is a five-hundred-dram coin from Armenia. At the time of its minting, it was just enough to buy a ride across town. This particular coin survived at least one war. I know, because a buddy of mine found it in the pocket of his great-great-great-great-great-great grandfather's army uniform."

The robot stared at it for a moment, cradled it close, then deposited it in a secret compartment similar to Taft's. "If you require anything else during your stay, Mr. Winder, please do not hesitate to ask."

"I won't." Croft patted one of its many shoulders, much gentler than Kaizon had pounded his, then started once again for the elevator.

A woman's tearful crying froze Croft in his tracks. He would recognize that voice anywhere. It belonged to the woman who had sent the nav program and saved their lives.

And it was coming from the docking port of Kaizon's ship.

He crept back to the docking ramp and peered down in time to see the robot disappear into the airlock, sealing the woman's heartbroken cries off with it.

Croft made it halfway down the ramp before common sense finally caught up with him. Boarding another ship without permission was illegal. Not only that, if the ship had automated defenses, it would have perfect legal precedent to shoot him dead if he tried to force entry. Even waiting outside its airlock was technically an arrestable offense — one the luggage robot would be obligated to report.

Gritting his teeth against the staggering injustice, Croft climbed back up, sat opposite the ramp, and waited.

Ten minutes later, the luggage bot still hadn't emerged.

Impatience gnawed at him. Croft had to know if she was all right. He pulled out his data pad, connected to *Majestic,* scrolled through the communication log, and hailed Kaizon's ship on the same channel he had been hailed when they'd exited the skipstream.

"Croft! I guess that's one way to reach me."

Sadly, it was Kaizon's voice.

"Where are you?" Kaizon said. "We're already halfway through our first round of drinks."

"We?"

"Yeah. Took a little asking around, but I eventually found your Maria."

Damnit. "I, ah … just wanted to let you know that I got held up, but I'll be there shortly."

"No rush, buddy. Maria and I are having a great chat. Isn't that right?"

"Right! Croft, did you know that Kaizon is a water trader? He says there might be an opportunity right here on the station. A big one! Isn't that fantastic?"

Croft's heart fell into his shoes. It was happening. Again.

But her unbridled enthusiasm made it hard for him to be upset. "Yeah, Maria, that's great. I'm happy for you." Strangely, he meant it.

"Your jiffy is up, by the way," Maria said. "I ordered a cocktail I think you're going to love. Come drink it before the ice melts."

Croft stared down the dock ramp, where the mystery woman's cries had echoed like a cavern of misery. "Look ... I'm, uh, still tied up here. Order me something tasty from the menu, would you? I'll see you in a bit."

Maria huffed. "That wouldn't *happen* to be because you have your tools out tinkering with the ship again, would it?"

"W-what? No! Maria —"

"Have fun doing whatever the hell it is you're doing, Croft!"

The connection died.

Croft put his face in his hands. Like the rest of this trip, that conversation hadn't gone at all the way he'd planned.

The airlock below opened. Croft jumped in guilty surprise, having momentarily forgotten why he'd been illegally hanging around Kaizon's ship. The multi-armed luggage bot walked up the ramp carrying only a few bags, many fewer than Taft had hauled out of Maria's ship.

"Hey there," Croft said, standing. "Sorry, I didn't get your name?"

"Bult."

"Great. How did everything go in there, Bult? Did you notice anything unusual?"

"Every ship has irregularities, Mr. Winder."

"Call me Croft, please."

"Very well. I am not at liberty to comment on guests' private property, including the contents of their luggage, or the interior of their ships."

"Not even if someone's life is in danger?"

"In that case, I am authorized to report my findings to Security, but I am restricted to relay only information pertinent to the endangered entity's circumstances."

"You didn't happen to report anything while you were inside Kaizon's ship, did you?"

"No." Bult tilted its binocular eyes. "Do you suspect someone inside the craft is in danger?"

Croft's mouth fell open, but he quickly clamped it shut. Robot empathy wasn't very acute — a fact he reminded himself of to keep from snapping at the luggage bot. "Bult, you *did* hear the woman crying when you entered the airlock, right?"

Bult considered for a second. "I heard crying."

"That usually means someone is distressed, possibly in danger. Did you investigate the source of the crying?"

"Yes. That is why my luggage retrieval took two hundred and sixteen percent longer than average."

"So ... she wasn't in danger?"

"Technically, I am not even allowed to answer that, but ... no, Mr. Winder, she was not in danger."

Croft relaxed, if only a little. "Can you tell me anything else about her? Anything at all?"

"I'm afraid not, unless you can produce evidence that her life is in imminent danger."

He couldn't. Croft pinched the bridge of his nose and sighed. "Look ... if it wasn't for that woman, you would be scraping my remains off the station's outer hull right now. I owe her my life, but I have no way of repaying her. Worse, it sounds like she's unhappy. Suffering. It ... it's killing me. I just want to help her somehow — show her a fraction of the kindness she's shown me."

Bult touched the compartment where it had stored Croft's coin. All six of its shoulders sagged.

Another compartment in its chest popped open. A small circuit board emerged and clattered to the ground.

"It is unfortunate that my communications module came loose," Taft said. "It contains the last channel I communicated on and, if misused, could compromise the privacy of that guest. Hopefully it is not recovered. If it is, I hope it is beyond repair, otherwise I will surely be subjected to disciplinary action."

Croft scooped it up and clutched it to his chest. "Bult, I ... I don't know what to say."

"Say that you will continue your behavior patterns during your stay, and it will have been worth the sacrifice."

"I will."

Bult tipped its head, then ambled toward the elevator, bags swinging like a luggage tree.

My behavior patterns?

Croft wasn't sure what Bult meant, but he had an inkling, and that was enough.

Gripping the precious communication module, he dashed back to *Majestic*, where his tools that Maria so despised awaited.

3

SAVIOR IN DISTRESS

CROFT PUT THE FINISHING TOUCHES on his makeshift cradle for the communications module Bult had so generously lost. He preferred working with larger components, but no ship mechanic worth their salt could escape being part electronic whiz. Most of the problems he fixed were caused by failed systems, which meant he'd had to either learn to work on circuitry, or close shop.

Tiny lights flickered on the module. Croft held his breath, fearing the worst, but no smoke appeared. Characters scrolled by on the screen next to it in a language he didn't recognize. He ran it through the translator, which confirmed his suspicion that it was simply a boot sequence, followed by a command prompt.

He was in.

Finding the commands to reconnect to the last caller was even easier, thanks to a readily accessible service manual on the manufacturer's product page. He entered them in, then stared at the speaker on the table, connected to the module by two, flimsy wires.

The speaker whined a familiar data connection tone.

"Hello?" Croft said. Odds were low that anyone would hear him through the data noise, but he had to try.

The whine ceased. "Hello?" a familiar female voice said.

Yes!

"Hi, this is Crofton —"

"Winder," the woman said. "Yes, I remember you. H-how are you communicating over this channel? It's usually reserved for ... other purposes."

Huh?

"Oh. Well, let's just say I was worried about you, and happened to make the right friend at the right time."

"You were worried about ... me?"

"Yes. I, ah, heard you crying earlier when passing by your docking ladder. Is everything okay?"

She laughed. "You stole some poor luggage bot's communication module just to make sure I was all right?"

How did she know that?

"W-well," Croft said, recovering his manners, "after what you did for us, it seemed the least I could do. Besides, I didn't steal it."

"Sure you didn't."

"It's true!"

"Just teasing." She laughed again. "Bult told me about the coin you tipped. That was very kind."

"Oh, it was nothing. And not to be rude, but you haven't answered my question. Are you okay?"

"I am now."

A smile spread across Croft's face, slow and sweet as honey. He cleared his throat, suddenly self-conscious that he was grinning like an idiot. "So, ah ... are you coming onto the station anytime soon?"

"No," she said softly. "I have to stay here."

The sadness in her voice broke Croft's heart. "Would you like a visitor?"

"I'd love one, but Kaizon would never allow it. He'd be furious to learn I'm even talking to you."

Invite me anyway, Croft wanted to say, but memory of Kaizon's powerful build and sharp teeth kept his brash response in check.

Which made Croft wonder what this woman looked like. Was she as burly as Kaizon? More so? Did she have the same deep-red skin? Or were the females of Kaizon's species completely different? Were she and Kaizon even the same species?

"Would you like me to disconnect?" Croft found himself saying instead. He couldn't bear the thought of making life worse for this poor woman.

"No." She took a deep, shuddering breath. "Tell me about yourself, Crofton Winder."

Now that's a boring topic.

"All right," he said anyway, glad she wanted to continue the conversation. "But only if you call me Croft."

"Then I guess this is goodbye. It was nice —"

"Wait! I-I was just trying to be friendly. Please don't disconnect."

Her laugh filled his small work area. "Got you, *Croft.*"

"Oh, you're a real riot." He grinned despite his pounding heart.

"So, are you going to tell me about yourself, or do I have to pull another mean trick to entertain myself?"

"Fine, but I won't be held responsible for any snoring my lackluster life story induces."

"You imply that I snore," the mysterious woman said.

"Do you?"

"Ack! Rude much?"

"So you *do* snore."

"I — *no!* Stop putting words in my mouth!"

"That's all right. I won't tell anyone."

"Croft! I swear I'm going to ..." She trailed off at his chuckle, then chuckled herself. "Bastard. The point goes to you. I guess we're even."

"Doesn't mean we have to stop playing, though, does it?"

"No, I suppose it doesn't."

"Good. Now, as for my riveting life story ..."

Croft kept it as short and interesting as possible. Born on Earth. Raised by two parents along with his younger sister. Always loved mechanical things. Apprenticed at one of the largest shipyards in the Tol Theta system. Opened a shop of his own, and made a modest living. Then he met ...

"Anyway, enough about me," Croft said, uncomfortable discussing the details of his current relationship with a complete stranger. "What about you?"

"Oh no you don't. Tell me about her. How did you meet?"

"I, ah ... Well, we met on the ski slopes of Edelon."

"In the Tau or Gredelon system?"

"Tau. You know it?"

"Definitely," she said. "They have the best space racecourse in the sector."

"You're a racing fan?"

"More than a fan. I'm a rally pilot."

"Get out!"

"No, really! I won the Karteit Asteroid Run two years in a row, among others."

Croft whistled low. "That course takes guts. And a craft that can turn on a dime."

"On a what?"

"Sorry. Outmoded Earthen term for a nimble vehicle."

"Ah, my translator missed that one. Yes, it's challenging, but I — my craft can handle it. It's capable of producing full primary thrust on any of the three axes simultaneously."

"Get out!"

"No, *you* get out," she said, laughing. "It's my ship!"

"No wonder you bagged the Karteit. I've never even heard of a ship with full-power omni-directional thrust."

And for good reason.

Croft could think of no faster way to plaster a pilot against the hull than instantaneous primary thrust in any direction.

"They didn't make many," she said. "Finding qualified mechanics is a challenge. The engine is marvel enough, but the inertia-absorbing cockpit throws off most mechanics. The entire thing moves in all axes to lessen the effects of sudden acceleration change on the pilot."

"Wow! I'd love to get my hands on this thing and see what's under the covers."

"Y-yes, um ..." She cleared her throat, a nervous edge in her voice. "I ... I'd like that, as long as you're gentle. It may be a racer, but it's still ... delicate."

Croft puzzled on her words, unsure if they were still talking about the ship. "Don't worry, I treat my crafts with the same care I would a person. More so, in some cases."

"I don't doubt that one bit. Sadly, it isn't my permission to give. You'd have to clear it with Kaizon. I'd ask him myself, but he won't even speak to me until he's back aboard."

"I'll do just that. He seems to like me. Maybe he'll agree to let me see your ship."

And you, Croft thought, more intrigued than ever about the skilled pilot on the other end of the comm link.

"Well, I won't hold my breath," she said, "but I do wish you luck. It would be nice to meet you in person."

"For sure. A proper 'thank you' for saving our lives can only be done face-to-face."

"Are you going to give me a coin, too, like you gave Taft and Bult?"

"No. A deed of that magnitude deserves something better. More personal."

"Oh? Now I'm intrigued. What is it?"

"I'm not sure yet. To pick a truly special gift, I'll first have to get to know you better."

"Well, then, here's hoping you can convince Kaizon to —"

A loud *zap* sounded from the communication module on his desk, followed by a cloud of smoke. Croft yanked it from the cradle he'd cobbled together, but black marks marred its surface. He knew a dead module when he saw one.

He sat back and gripped his hair in great bunches.

That module had been his only means of communicating with the woman trapped on Kaizon's ship. Even if he somehow obtained another, he didn't know the channel, nor did he have the authorization codes necessary to re-establish a connection.

Worse, he still didn't know her name.

He gathered himself, then cleaned up his mess and headed for the airlock. Kaizon awaited him at The Restaurant, and Croft was suddenly *very* eager to speak with him.

4

MISUNDERSTOOD

VIDEO WALKTHROUGHS of the Truck Stop at the Center of the Galaxy had failed to convey what awaited Croft when he stepped out of the elevator to the Main Ring.

The station was, in a word, enormous. The ceiling soared seventy meters overhead — so high that looking up gave him vertigo. The ring spanned just as far across, having room for several city blocks between. Lengthwise ... Croft had read that jogging completely around the Main Ring was a staggering eight-kilometer run. One-quarter of that — the Orange Quadrant — was apparently off-limits, but Croft intended to explore every nook and cranny that wasn't. Delphian technology was extremely rare and difficult to decipher. To have discovered an entire *station* of it was beyond every tech geek's dream.

And so, Croft found the mostly human technology surrounding him disappointing. Buildings, benches, lights, and artwork all smacked of Earthen origin. Croft had hoped to step out of the elevator into a completely alien environment. Instead, he found himself walking in an enclosed version of his home planet. The station had been severely damaged when Zed's company had discovered it thirty-five years ago. Extensive reconstruction had left little of its original design intact.

But the heaviness in his chest, he realized, wasn't because of that. Croft had come here with the intention of enjoying the station's wonders with Maria. To create a shared experience that might bring them together.

Yet here he was, marveling his first glimpse of this alien relic, alone.

How had Maria reacted when she'd stepped off the elevator? Had she gasped? Or had she been too engrossed in her data pad to notice?

Croft swore under his breath. If only the autopilot hadn't failed, or if he'd remembered to affix the luggage locators, he might be dining with her right now, planning out the rest of their trip on this glorious station.

Instead, Maria was dining with Kaizon.

Croft hurried to a transportation tube. A green arrow pointed left, which he assumed meant it was going spinwise toward the Green Quadrant. He pressed the call button near the loading hatch.

A series of pops and squeaks sounded behind him, which Croft's ear communicator quickly translated.

"Oi, mate! This tube go to the Green Quadrant?" For whatever reason, the translator had chosen a male voice with a rough, British accent.

"Sure does," Croft said without turning around, still distracted in thought. He pointed at the green arrow.

"Thanks. You think they'd code these things for races who can't see color. Blooming owners just assume everyone's eyes work same as theirs. Those that have eyes, that is. Damned inconsiderate, if you ask me."

Croft turned to find a large, stick-like figure staring back at him with beady black eyes. Lights glared from its shiny yellow carapace like miniature suns, making Croft squint.

Quick as a whip, the creature punched him in the face.

Croft staggered against the tube, holding his nose. He hadn't heard a *crunch,* but that didn't mean it wasn't broken.

"Ow! What the hell was that for?"

"Sorry, mate! I didn't mean to —"

Croft glanced between his fingers, only to see a yellow fist flying at him again. His head smacked against the tube with a loud *clung!* The world spun. Croft fell to his knees, struggling to stay upright.

"Sorry again! Keep your eyes down, mate, or you might get another wallop."

"Or you could just *stop punching me!*"

"Wish it were that easy. I —"

Without realizing it, Croft had met the creature's eyes again. The yellow fist flew at him a third time. Dizzy or not, adrenaline put Croft on the defensive. He jerked aside and narrowly avoided another wallop. The creature's fist *clanged* against the tube.

"Yikes!" It spun in a full circle, cradling its hand. "That smarts something awful."

"Then stop doing it!"

"Can't! It's reflex. My species shows aggression by exposing the whites of our eyes. Unfortunately, you Earthens show your whites all the time."

Which genius allowed you onto a predominantly Earthen station, then?

"Sounds like quite a tic," Croft said instead. He kept his eyes down this time, although his good manners nagged him for being rude.

"'tis. We've mostly overcome it as a species. Only one in a thousand of us still carry that gene. For those who do, though, the compulsion is irresistible."

"You're one of the lucky winners, it seems."

"Yeah. Sorry again, mate. Wouldn't have even come to this station if it weren't for pressing business." It knelt before him. "Here, close your eyes and let me see the mess."

Croft did so.

"Ugh. I'm guessing the skin on your cheek isn't supposed to be split open and leaking?"

"Red liquid?"

"Wouldn't know. Can't see in color, mate."

Croft bowed his head, careful to avert his gaze. Sure enough, blood covered his fingers. "No, it definitely isn't supposed to look like that."

Worse, I can't show up to dinner looking like I just lost a fight.

"Any idea where the medical ward is?" Croft said.

"Not a clue. But don't you worry, I'll see you there safely."

"Thanks, I really —"

Manners once again overrode Croft's sense of self-preservation. He met the creature's beady eyes, intending to express his gratitude.

A carapace-covered fist whacked his face. This time, the world went black.

•   •   •

Croft slowly opened his eyes to the glare of overhead lights. His head pounded. His cheek throbbed. His right eye wouldn't quite open all the way.

"Oi, doctor! I think he's awake."

Croft glanced over, too late remembering that was a bad idea, but a makeshift cloth covered the yellow creature's eyes.

"There we go," the yellow creature said. "Should prevent me from clobbering you again." It reached a hand out and blindly patted Croft's arm. "Glad you're okay, mate. Gave me a right scare, you did."

"Couldn't have that," Croft said dryly. He tried to sit up, but a wave of dizziness made him settle back down. "How long have I been out?"

"An hour. Doc kept you under a few minutes extra to stitch you up. Proper job, that is. Bloke knows what he's doing."

"Got a mirror?"

The creature lifted its blindfold. Croft kept his eyes averted while it searched around, then it handed over a shiny metal plate. While not exactly a mirror, it was clear enough for Croft to see the thin red line running up his cheek. By itself, the wound gave him the air of a rugged sword fighter. Combined with dark bruises, however, he looked like nothing more than a thug. Maria would not be pleased.

Maria!

Croft struggled to his feet, ignoring the dizziness. "I've got to get to The Restaurant!"

"What, with all those body fluids on your shirt? Don't know about your planet, mate, but on mine that's considered unappetizing. Wouldn't even let me in the door looking like that."

Croft glanced down. Sure enough, red spattered his shirt. Even if The Restaurant let him in, Maria would throw a fit. She hated when Croft made her look bad in social situations — which he seemed to excel at.

"Thanks for the advice. I'm Croft, by the way."

"I'm —"

Croft's translator balked at whatever series of squeaks and clicks the creature made.

"Hecklesnort," the translator said eventually.

Hecklesnort?

Communicators did their best, but they sometimes translated too literally. In this case, Croft would save the creature's dignity and *not* use that name in public. He replaced the word "Hecklesnort" in his translation program with "Eckle," which seemed fitting for the amusing if violent creature and its Cockney accent.

"Pleased to meet you," Croft said. "Well, Eckle, you're absolutely right. I'm in no shape for a fancy dinner. Unless, of course, the doctor has a spare shirt and makeup kit handy."

"I don't." A man in a white lab coat walked over and peered down with serious brown eyes. "Eckle, as you call him, did quite a number on you. I'm obligated to ask if you wish to press charges?"

Eckle is a him? I guess the doctor would know.

Croft glanced at the blindfolded figure beside him. Red tufts of what looked like miniature trees protruded from the top of his head, swaying to some ethereal breeze. Other than that, he sat perfectly still.

And he went through the trouble of bringing me here, it seems.

"No, it was a simple misunderstanding," Croft said. "Mostly on my part. I'll be more careful in the future. And thank you for the stitches, doctor. Excellent job all around."

"You're welcome, but credit where credit's due. I provided directions, but my assistant performed the work."

The doctor gestured behind him to a pile of scrap metal. Croft jumped when the pile moved. The squat robot stood only as tall as the doctor's navel. Four limbs attached with various medical-looking instruments hung at its sides. One limb swung uselessly. The robot limped over, squeaking with every step, and bowed its shiny, bowl-like head.

"I am glad you are well," the squat medical robot said in a surprisingly natural voice. "I used invisi-sutures and liquid skin to seal your laceration, which went quite deep, but I could do little about your bruise. My apologies if that interferes with your evening plans."

"No apologies necessary. Like I said, top-notch job." Croft scratched his head and winced when his fingers touched a sore spot. He turned to the doctor. "No offense, but your assistant looks like it could use some medical care itself."

"None taken," the doctor said. "I'm as upset as anyone, truth be told. Quaxlig is an excellent assistant, and would be even more so if it had full use of its limbs."

"So what's the problem? Short on cash?"

"Short on skilled repair personnel." The doctor gave a wry grin. "As you may have noticed, the station's reconstruction is far from complete. Many core systems are still touch-and-go, which keeps the service crew busy 'round-the-clock. Any repairs not deemed critical are on indefinite hold." He patted the little bot's domed head. "Bad as it looks, Quaxlig is still functional, which means it may not receive service for quite some time. Years, perhaps."

"That's horrible," Croft said, mostly to himself.

He motioned the squat robot closer, who ambled forward. Croft inspected its dead arm. He immediately spotted the broken linkage, easily repairable with a welding kit. The squeak in its leg, on closer inspection, had the unmistakable sound of grinding bearings.

"Wait right here."

Croft stood. The station swam around him, however, and he fell against the bed. The doctor and Quaxlig rushed to his aid. After a few seconds, the station steadied.

"Thanks. I'm all right."

"Bollocks you are," Eckle said. "Have a quick kip, mate. Your bird will understand."

Croft pressed his lips together to keep from laughing. Whoever claimed translation programmers had no sense of humor obviously hadn't spoken to a … well, whatever Eckle was.

"No, really, I'll be fine," Croft said. "I just need help getting to my ship to fetch a few things, then I'll be right back."

"If there's no talking you out of it, I'll walk you there."

Eckle started to remove his blindfold. Croft needed no reminders, apart from his throbbing face, to look away.

On the walk back to the great spoke, where the elevators led down to the Docking Ring, Croft gathered his courage and called Maria.

"Croft! Where have you been? We're just finishing dessert. Your meal is long cold."

"Sorry, Maria. I had a bit of an accident. Afraid I'm in no shape for dinner."

"What happened?"

"Hit my face against something hard."

"I'm sure." Maria's voice dripped acid. "You were working on that damned ship again, weren't you?"

"Not this time."

"I should have known," she said, as if he hadn't spoken. "Well, don't worry about me. Kaizon filled me in on the trade opportunity at the station. He has an idea of how we might work together to win the contract. We have plenty to discuss this evening, so you just keep ... *tinkering,* or whatever the hell it is you're doing!"

"Don't be like that," Croft said gently. "Give me a chance to freshen up, then I'll meet you at The Restaurant. We can take a walk along the observation deck, or grab a drink. Whatever you want to do."

"We'll see." She heaved a dramatic sigh. "It's been a long day."

"I'll take that as a 'maybe' and hope for the best."

To his great surprise — and pleasure — she gave a small laugh. "Get some rest, and don't injure yourself overmuch. And if you do join us, wear something presentable. Kaizon may introduce us to some of his business associates later."

Why am I not surprised?

"Of course, dear. I know just the outfit. See you soon."

Croft ended the call.

Eckle clicked and rattled in a rhythmic cadence that Croft's translator confirmed as a laugh. "Can't believe you're trusting your bird to Kaizon, mate!"

"You know him?"

"Everyone in the water trade does. Ruthless, he is. Nothing he won't do to win a deal."

Croft paused in mid-step. "Ruthless? He wouldn't hurt Maria, would he?"

"Nah, not ruthless like that. But he might well swipe her out from under you, if you know what I mean. Especially if it benefits his trade. She doesn't go for the maned, toothy types, does she?"

"I, ah … I don't think so."

At least, I hope not.

Just in case, Croft dashed the last few meters to the elevator and pressed the call button, then again and again.

"You're still going back to the medical ward first?" Eckle said.

"Yes." Croft stepped into the elevator, waited for Eckle, then mashed the bottom button. "I have to trust that Maria can take care of herself for a little while."

"But why? Your med expenses are all paid, fair and square."

"It isn't about that. Quaxlig fixed me up. I'm nowhere near as good a robot mechanic as it is a surgeon, but I'm sure I can repair Quaxlig well enough to last through its next maintenance cycle."

"Ain't your problem, mate. But Kaizon is."

Croft took a long, measured breath. "If Kaizon can woo her away from me in a single evening, then Maria and I have bigger problems than just him."

"Sounds a bit fatalistic," Eckle said.

Maybe it is, Croft thought, *my subconscious telling me to finally face the fact that we're a lost cause.*

He shook his head. Their getaway vacation had only just begun. He couldn't give up without at least trying.

On the Docking Ring, Croft paused at the ramp leading down to Kaizon's ship — and to the mystery woman trapped inside. He had no way of contacting her, short of banging on the airlock, which she probably wouldn't have heard anyway. Reluctantly, he tore his eyes away and continued to his own docking ramp.

"Nice ship," Eckle said once they were inside *Majestic.* "Yours?"

"No, it's Maria's. And thanks. Except for the autopilot program, it's a very nice ship."

"What happened to the autopilot?"

"Not sure. It failed sometime before we came out of stasis. We nearly cratered against the station."

"So that was you."

Croft did a double-take. Eckle's pops and squeaks had been

much softer, as if talking to himself, but the translator had repeated it at full volume.

"Sorry, mate," Eckle said in a normal tone. "Word is that a ship almost collided with the station coming hot out of skipstream. Didn't know that was you."

"It was. And, given what we just heard, it could be a while before station technicians get around to fixing it. I don't suppose you have a spare autopilot module laying around?"

"I do, in fact. Send me the access codes to your ship. I'll have me boys come around tonight and see what they can do."

"You will?" Croft blushed at the incredibly generous offer. "I ... I don't know what to say."

"You already said it by *not* pressing assault charges. Least I can do for you, mate."

"Oh. Well, thanks then."

"No problem. So, what we here for?"

"Tools."

Croft grabbed the backpack containing his equipment, then put an empty pack on the table and started loading spare parts: rods, wires, bolts, extra solder, and other things that looked useful. Quaxlig was in bad shape; its arm and leg probably weren't its only components in need of repair. The replacement parts didn't have to fit perfectly, just perfectly enough.

He hefted the part-laden bag onto his shoulder. Its weight nearly toppled him over.

"Here, let me get that." Eckle grabbed the heavy bag. He seemed to struggle just as much as Croft with the weight, but managed to sling it over his shoulder. "Ready?"

"As soon as I grab a change of clothes for later. These are already ruined, so they'll be fine for repair work."

"Sure, I'll be outside."

After retrieving the outfit he'd bought for his first high-society shindig with Maria — the one and only set of nice clothing Croft owned — he and Eckle made their way back to the medical ward.

Quaxlig and the doctor seemed surprised to see them. They appeared even more surprised when Croft opened his bag and began pulling out tools.

"Stand over there," Croft said to Quaxlig, pointing next to a metal stool.

Quaxlig obeyed. Croft sat on the stool, gently took the robot's non-functioning arm, and set to work.

Unfortunately, Croft had been right about the robot's sorry state. After welding the broken rod in Quaxlig's arm, then replacing the bearing in its leg, he made the mistake of asking if the little robot required any other maintenance. Two hours and a lot of improvised replacement parts later, Croft could honestly say he'd done everything he could.

The results were worth it. Quaxlig glided across the floor with the grace of a true surgeon — and without a squeak to be heard. It flexed and spun its multi-tooled arms as if they were brand new, and even did a little twirl.

"Many thanks, Mr. Winder," Quaxlig said. "My next patients should thank you, too."

"My pleasure, Quaxlig."

Croft checked the time and groaned. Maria had been waiting for him at The Restaurant for over three hours now. He wouldn't be surprised if she and Kaizon had already left. Even Eckle, who'd been a fixture at Croft's side, had made a quiet exit sometime during the repairs.

"If you need anything else while I'm at the station," Croft said to Quaxlig, packing the last of his tools, "you know how to reach me."

"Oh, there is one other thing, Mr. Winder."

Croft suppressed another groan. He really wanted to catch Maria to see if he could salvage any part of the evening, but walking out on the little robot would be rude. Instead, he smiled. "Yes?"

"A message arrived in my inbox while you were working on me, which, as luck might have it, appears to be for you. May I forward it to you?"

Croft puzzled on that. Why would someone send a message through Quaxlig — a bot he'd only just met — instead of directly to him?

"Um, sure," Croft said, more curious than anything.

The message arrived milliseconds later through an application Croft rarely used: an encrypted chat platform meant for anonymous communications, mostly by teenagers who wanted to be sneaky. The subject and return address were blank, which was typical for this platform. The body read, "Guess who?" followed by an image of an asteroid. Below it sat a series of characters he couldn't make sense of.

"Quaxlig, any idea what these symbols mean?"

"No. Sorry, Mr. Winder." A small slot opened on Quaxlig's chest. Out popped a familiar-looking module, which Quaxlig pressed into Croft's hand. "I have no idea what those codes mean, and they are most certainly not programmed into this communication module, which I seem to have misplaced. Fortunately, communication modules are classified as critical components, so I should have no trouble obtaining another. Have a pleasant evening, Mr. Winder."

Croft's heart leaped. That message had to be from the mystery woman on Kaizon's ship.

"Wait!"

Quaxlig turned to him.

"You, ah ... don't happen to have an interface for this module lying around, do you? My last patch job fizzled."

Quaxlig searched briefly, then shook its head. "These modules are not intended for use by organics. However, a robot repair shop might have diagnostic equipment that would meet your needs."

"Thanks!"

Croft left the medical ward at a run — but not toward the repair shop. As much as the mysterious woman on Kaizon's ship worried him, his girlfriend had waited too long already.

After all, if he couldn't fix his own relationship, then by what prayer — and by what right — did he believe he could help anyone else?

5

JILTED

CROFT FOUND THE RESTAURANT by asking directions from a friendly cleaning robot, whom he'd tipped with a coin and a brief story.

Unfortunately, Maria had already left.

He pulled out his data pad to call her, but a familiar series of pops and clicks caught his attention, followed by a Cockney voice from his translator.

"Oi! There you are, mate."

Eckle hurried down the walkway toward Croft, who stood like a goof with his finger over the "Connect" button on his data pad. Croft quickly lowered his gaze to avoid eye contact.

"I suspected they'd left without you," Eckle said. "And I was right."

"Who had?" Croft said, though he had a sinking feeling he knew.

"Kaizon and your bird. I sent me boys around to install the replacement autopilot, like I promised, except your ship weren't there."

"Wasn't ..." Croft paled. "H-how do you know Kaizon's with her?"

"Because I know that crafty git. Give her a shout, mate. I'll eat me" — the translator blanked — "if I'm wrong."

Since Croft had been about to do that anyway, he swallowed his apprehension and called Maria.

"Croft! Where are you?"

"I could ask you the same thing."

"Yes, well, we got tired of waiting for you at The Restaurant, so we stopped by our room, then checked the ship, but you were nowhere to be found. I figured you were off playing with some alien technical gizmo or other. Heaven knows there are enough of them around here."

"So you decided to take *Majestic* on a joy ride with Kaizon?" *Instead of calling me?*

"It isn't a joy ride! I told Kaizon about the performance modifications you made to the ship. He was impressed, and wanted to take it out for a spin to see for himself. I didn't think you'd mind. And ... how did you know I was out with Kaizon?"

"A little bird told me."

Croft gave Eckle a grateful nod, careful not to meet his eyes. The "little" part was an exaggeration, but he really did remind Croft of a tall, spindly, featherless bird. Who punched people. Hard.

"Maria, are you sure it's a good idea to take the ship out? You'll need the autopilot to dock, and we still don't know why it glitched in the first place."

"We ran into some technicians when we arrived at the docking ramp. They were just finishing up, and said everything looks okay for now, so we decided to take a chance."

Kaizon growled something, which Croft's earpieces quickly translated. "Hey buddy! Gotta say, this is one sweet ride. You must be one helluva mechanic."

"Oh, well ... thank you. I did put a bit of work into it."

"More than a bit," Maria said. "I bought it as a fixer-upper. I wouldn't have purchased it in the first place, but Croft swore he could turn it into a winner, so I caved. In the end, he was right, and saved me a lot of money."

"I bet," Kaizon said. "Good mechanics are hard to find. Great mechanics, impossible. And to be sleeping with one! I don't suppose there's room in your bed for me, too?" He barked a loud, hearty laugh.

Croft found it not the least bit amusing, not while the two of them were alone together on a ship with a double bed.

It wasn't that he didn't trust Maria; he sincerely doubted red, toothy, dog-like aliens were her type. But, if Eckle had spoken truly, he had reason to believe that Maria might very well be Kaizon's type. And in more ways than one.

Croft gulped his nervousness down and forced himself to sound calm. "So, when might you two be back?"

"That depends," Maria said, her voice sparking like struck flint. "When are *you* going to be done doing … whatever the hell it is you're tinkering with?"

He started to deny that he'd been tinkering, but it would have been a lie. Regardless of how badly Quaxlig had needed his help, Croft *had* been tinkering. Given the opportunity to do it over, he would make the same choice again.

Just like Maria had made her choice.

"Take your time," Croft said. "I have enough to keep me occupied for a while."

The words pained him to say. He wanted to be with Maria, but it also stung that she had not only gone off without him, but had chosen someone else's company, and done so in a manner where he couldn't follow. He needed time to get his head straight before confronting her, or he might end up saying something he would regret.

"Fine, we will!" Maria's heated voice could easily have been mistaken for one of Kaizon's growls. "Goodbye, Croft!"

Only after the line went dead did Croft realize his colossal mistake. Maria had been reaching out to him. She'd practically begged him to say he was done, and that he wanted her to come back. But he couldn't, no more than she could apologize for leaving with Kaizon without even bothering to call Croft first.

Stubbornness abounded on both sides, exacerbated by a year of trying to make a relationship work that, perhaps, was doomed to fail from the very start.

Unless they both made an effort to change, it undoubtedly would.

"Sorry, mate," Eckle said. "Wish I weren't right about Kaizon, but at least you know now rather than him sweeping her away sometime later with only a note of goodbye."

"Maria can take care of herself," Croft said, although emotion wrangled his throat in a vice grip, pressed against his lungs, and crushed his heart. "You said Kaizon isn't physically aggressive, and she's *very* good at saying no."

"Assuming she wants to say no."

"There's that." Croft rubbed his face. He didn't want to think about it. He didn't want to think about anything.

Except he had to. Kaizon and Maria running away together didn't just affect him. Someone else needed to know.

"Would … would you excuse me, Eckle? I need to run to the repair shop for a … an errand."

"'course, mate. Do what you gotta do. I still recommend replacing that autopilot, though, so let me know when they're back and I'll send me boys around again."

"Sure. What's your galactic address?"

After exchanging contact information and a few test messages, Croft bid Eckle farewell and made his way to the transportation tubes.

The repair shop, it turned out, was located on the opposite side of the station in the Red Quadrant. Croft had discovered this by asking a pair of friendly robots, who had practically fought each other in their eagerness to give him directions. He'd thanked them by tipping each with a coin and a story. The pair had scurried off with their treasures as if they'd won the robot lottery, leaving Croft, smiling, to take the two-kilometer ride to the other side of the Main Ring.

The long line of customers outside the repair shop shouldn't have surprised Croft, but it did. Humans, aliens, robots, and androids alike stood with varying degrees of patience. Some gazed like zombies at their data pads. Some fidgeted. Some cradled their ailing devices. Some, sadly, *were* the ailing device.

Croft shuffled to the end of the line behind a two-legged robot listing to its left. The robot did a double-take and turned its square head around to face him.

"Crofton Winder?"

"That's me," he said, taken aback by the unexpected notoriety. "And you are?"

"Roxxak." It extended a three-fingered hand, which Croft shook. "You do not need to wait in line, Mr. Winder. Proceed to the front. A robot with green eyes will see to your needs."

"Really?" Croft glanced at the customers in front of him. There had to be fifteen at least. "That seems a little unfair. Are you sure?"

In answer, every robot and android in line nodded agreement. The organics seemed surprised or dismayed, but kept quiet.

"I ... well, okay."

Normally, Croft wouldn't have even entertained the idea, but his communication with the woman on Kaizon's ship was time-sensitive. He didn't want her to be caught by surprise when they returned — or if Kaizon didn't return at all. He also wanted the news to come from him instead of some stranger who might blurt it out and leave her to wallow in misery. Croft, at least, could offer some small comfort, if only in mutual commiseration.

Every eye watched him pass, prickling the back of his neck. Croft ignored them as best he could, squeezed past a squat blue alien holding what looked like a blender, and entered the shop. More eyes greeted him inside, some welcoming, some annoyed ...

... and one pair green.

The green-eyed robot was one of three bots attending the counter, along with a grizzled man with black-stained hands and a weathered face. The man looked up from the gadget he held and narrowed his eyes on Croft. He started to say something, but the green-eyed robot spoke over him.

"Mr. Hennessey, I am taking my break now. Mr. Winder is an honored guest at the station. If it is all right, I would like to show him around your esteemed shop."

"He wants to see the grimy back of a repair shop? Whatever for?"

"Oh, I'm a mechanic by trade," Croft said, hoping he understood the green-eyed robot's intent. "I never pass an opportunity to see the tools of a master craftsman."

"Mechanic?" The grizzled man laughed. "Don't say that too loud. They'll conscript you, they will. Make you open another shop like mine, or put you to work in the overloaded repair docks."

"Neither of those sound terrible. You seem to be doing well for yourself, Mr. Hennessey."

"Paul, please. And I'd be doing well if there were five more of me. The line you see here never ends, no matter the time of day. I have to take stimulants just to keep up."

"Perhaps I could stop by later to lend a hand."

Paul's gray-whiskered face broke into a grin. "You're either a fool, or you truly love your trade. Either way, I won't look a gift bot in the solenoids if you're set on helping, though I'm surprised you don't have anything better to do."

Depends on when Maria returns, and whose room she decides to sleep in tonight.

"If I can wrangle a few free hours, you'll be the first to know."

"I won't wait up, then." Paul waved him in the general direction of the door behind the counter, then returned his attention to the gizmo in his hands, and the anxious customer it belonged to.

The green-eyed bot led him into the back room, which looked exactly as Croft expected. Tools, drawers, and drawers with tools covered every wall. Two full racks of labeled components represented the work backlog, which had overflowed to a pile on the floor.

Curiously, the workbenches were unoccupied, as was the rest of the back room, leaving Croft and the green-eyed robot all the privacy they needed.

"This is the device you seek, Mr. Winder." The green-eyed robot pointed at a small cradle hooked up to a screen, then held out its fine, eight-fingered hand. "Allow me to connect the communication module for you, then I shall leave you in peace."

Croft handed it over. "Thank you ...?"

"Orquir." It gave a small bow, bending at hips above short continuous treads for feet.

"Orquir, I don't mean to sound ungrateful, but why are you doing this for me?"

Orquir looked up at him, green eyes flashing. "Kindness begets kindness, Mr. Winder. You have shown generosity to several artificial lifeforms already. Word travels at the speed of light among us, and the rumor is that your generosity continues."

It hooked the communication module up. Familiar characters flashed across the screen. Orquir gestured to the workbench and stepped away.

"I shall return from my break in thirteen minutes, forty-eight seconds. Please continue to be kind, Mr. Winder. Especially now."

Croft tugged the bot to a halt before it left, then pulled a coin from his pocket. "Can't leave without a tip, Orquir. Not after the kindness you've shown me."

Orquir rolled back to him without argument and gazed down at the coin. Sixteen fingers clacked against each other in rhythmic anticipation.

"This is a shilling, otherwise known as a five-pence."

Orquir accepted the dull, silvery coin with reverent fingers, then looked up at Croft, obviously awaiting its story.

"This one has a more tragic tale than most," Croft said. "It once belonged to a fisherman's wife in England. Rumor has it, this was the first coin their family had earned. She kept it through fifty-plus years of marriage, until illness claimed him, and she had spent every last penny keeping herself well in her old age. Every penny except this one, which her children found in a glass case when she died, along with a note detailing the family's history. I have an electronic copy and can send it along, if you like."

"Oh, yes please!"

Orquir shuddered. For a moment, Croft feared it might shake itself apart, but then it wheeled in a circle and held the coin up high.

"Thank you, Mr. Winder! Thank you so much!"

Clutching the coin to its chest, Orquir wheeled into the front room and closed the door behind it, leaving Croft alone with the powered communication module.

"That was so sweet," a familiar voice said from the speaker.

"What? Oh! I-I didn't know you were already connected."

"As I suspect Orquir intended," the mysterious woman on Kaizon's ship said, laughing. "I'm glad you received my message. How are you, Croft?"

"Well, um ... frankly, I've been better."

"What happened?"

Croft told her what he knew. When he finished, silence hung over them, thick as tar, until she finally spoke in a cracked, strained voice.

"Kaizon left the station with another woman on a ... a different ship?"

"I'm sorry," Croft said, momentarily forgetting his own pain. "It's my fault. If I'd returned to Maria sooner, this might never have happened."

"Yes, and if you'd maybe turned right down that hallway when you were a boy instead of left, you might now be president of the galaxy. Don't put responsibility for their actions on your shoulders, Croft." Her voice dropped to a whisper. "It isn't healthy, believe me. 'What if?' is a game you can't win."

"I'll try to remember that," Croft said earnestly. "It's hard, though. I've been doing it all my life."

"As have I. I still do, to be honest, but I'm getting better at recognizing when I'm going down that path."

"Playing 'What if?' isn't always bad. In a sense, it's the only way we get better. 'If I had done this instead of that, then the outcome might have been more positive.' Then you try that thing and see what happens."

"You know, you're right, and I'm going to put that into practical application this minute." She took a deep breath. "Croft, are you still interested in paying me a visit?"

His heart jumped with a mixture of excitement and trepidation. Even from their brief conversations, he knew he'd get along with her well. They had similar interests. Their philosophies scarily aligned. They both suffered the same heartache. And, above all, he had no trouble talking to her.

On the other hand, he would effectively be doing the same thing that Maria had done to him, which the mysterious woman would also be doing to Kaizon. He couldn't stomach the thought of committing such blatant retaliation.

"Y-yes," Croft found himself saying anyway. "Very."

A part of him railed at the impropriety, but a bigger part — the piece of him hurting the most — didn't care. Croft had come to this station to be with someone special. Had spent his life savings on it, for Heaven's sake.

If Maria could fly off with someone else, then so could he.

"Great," the mysterious woman said, although she sounded less confident than before. "I-I can't open the hatch for you myself, but I'll give you Kaizon's access code."

She rattled off a long series of digits, which Croft punched into his data pad.

"Thanks. I'm only a quadrant away, so I'll be there in about fifteen minutes."

"Wonderful, that will give me time to freshen up." Her voice became soft again, unsure, as if she were shrinking in upon herself. "See you soon. And ..."

"What is it?"

"N-never mind. Just ... looking forward to meeting you in person."

"Same here. Maybe then you'll tell me your name."

"Maybe." Although Croft had no idea what she looked like, he could vividly imagine her impish grin. "Goodbye, Croft."

"Goodbye."

The connection closed. Croft stared at the screen for a few seconds, then disconnected the communication module, put it in his pocket, and collapsed into a chair with his head in his hands.

What am I doing?

But he already knew the answer. Croft didn't want to be alone. He would go where he could commiserate with the only other person on the station who understood.

He stood, took a deep breath, and headed for the exit.

If nothing else, he couldn't wait to find out what Kaizon's mysterious woman looked like.

6

MEETING

T HE ACCESS HATCH TO KAIZON'S SHIP loomed large and intimidating. Croft tucked the box of dried something-or-other fruits he'd purchased on the way over, which rattled like rocks, under his arm. The android at the gift shop, Rhoda, had assured him they were a Krurgik delicacy, although Croft still didn't know if the mysterious woman was Kaizon's race, or something completely different.

Either way, Croft had been raised to never come empty-handed to a get-together. Steadying his nerves, Croft punched the access code into the security pad.

The hatch whirred open. A *whoosh* of air equalized pressure between the airlock and Kaizon's ship, bringing with it pungent odors reminiscent of blue cheese and cigar smoke. Croft covered his nose and allowed a few seconds for his senses to adapt. When the smell no longer felt overpowering, he stepped inside.

The interior was smaller than even *Majestic's.* Or what he could see of it, anyway. Croft let his eyes adjust to the low light, then climbed into the ship.

Docked by its nose, the station's rotation made gravitational "up" toward the bow. Below, the aft of the ship ended abruptly in a sealed door. Above him sat a large cockpit, out through which he could see only the hull of the Docking Ring.

He did *not,* however, see anyone even resembling a humanoid.

"C-come in," a familiar voice said from the cockpit.

Croft tucked the fruit box in the back of his pants and climbed the ladder.

A figure sat waiting for him on what was technically the rear wall of the cockpit, shrouded in dark gray robes that hid her face.

"H-hi there," the mysterious woman said, waving a gloved hand.

She sounded strange in that she *didn't* sound strange, not like Croft would have expected an alien to sound.

Then he realized why. Her words hadn't come through his translator. The woman spoke English, and spoke it well.

Croft extended his hand. "Hi, it's a pleasure to finally meet you in person ...?"

"And you."

She either hadn't picked up on his unspoken prompt for her name, or had intentionally avoided answering. Croft suspected the latter. Her gloved hand shook his with the lightest of touches, then she tucked it back into the sleeve of her robe.

"Please, make yourself comfortable," she said. "And help yourself to the refreshments."

She gestured to a chair next to her. An assortment of snacks covered a box-table between them, none of which Croft recognized, along with a decanter of red liquid and two cups. The arrangement struck him as simple and delightful.

"Unfortunately, I can only offer Krurgik cuisine. Research shows it's digestible by humans, though I can't vouch for how it will taste."

"That's fine, I'm always up for an adventure. And this is for you."

Croft untucked the box of snacks from his waistband and handed it over. She accepted it with hesitant fingers, then placed it in her lap and simply stared down. Croft wished he could see her face so he'd have some inkling of her reaction. Was it not to her liking? Had he offended her somehow?

Slowly, she lifted the box and cradled it to her chest. Her shoulders shook briefly, as if she were quietly sobbing.

"Are ... are you all right?"

"I'm perfect," she said in a quavering voice. "Thank you, Croft. I don't remember the last time I received a gift. I forgot how wonderful it feels."

"Kaizon doesn't give you gifts? Is that a Krurgik thing?"

"No and no, but don't judge him for it. He does plenty for me, in his own way. More than he should have to."

"Including locking you in a ship while he traipses off with another woman?"

She fanned herself with the snack box, rattling its contents. "Oh boy. This isn't going at all as I'd imagined."

Croft paled. His father would have read him the galactic riot act for being so rude to a host. Her relationship with Kaizon was evidently more complicated than he'd guessed — and absolutely none of his business, unless she chose to bring it up.

"Sorry," Croft said. "My frustration with my own relationship got the best of me. I have no right to project onto you or Kaizon. What I would love is to learn more about this wonderful ship of yours."

"Of Kaizon's, you mean. And I'll forgive you. This time."

The humor in her voice made it easy to imagine her grinning beneath her robe. Croft delighted to hear the easy confidence that had been so prominent during their radio conversations.

"As for the ship," she said, "it's a limited edition. This is the last of its series in active service." The mysterious woman gestured around her. "The interior is actually a ship within a ship. The outer ship is twice the diameter of the inner one, which is electromagnetically suspended in the center."

"So when dramatic thrust is applied in any direction, the inner ship moves to lessen the effect on the passengers." Croft shook his head in wonder. "I can't imagine how much power that requires."

"A lot, which is why this ship is primarily used for short-course races. It does have a cruise mode, where the inner ship locks into place with physical restraints, but —"

"Where's the fun in that?" Croft finished for her.

She laughed. "Exactly! Doing so enacts severe throttling protocols to prevent enthusiastic pilots from splattering themselves against the viewport. Sure, cruise mode is more energy-efficient, but if you bought a racer like this, why would you ever?"

"Oh, I can think of a few reasons. You mentioned that mechanics qualified to service this ship are difficult to find. Pushing any racer to its limits is hard on its structure and systems, which is why most racing teams have dedicated mechanics. I'm guessing Kaizon doesn't."

She shook her head and sighed. "Which is probably why I haven't been in a proper race for such a long time."

"Probably."

"But I usually win! The prize money should at least cover the costs, shouldn't it?"

"Depends on how expensive your mechanic is, the price of materials, and what class you're racing in. Doesn't Kaizon share financial information with you?"

"No. He doesn't want me to worry so I can focus on being the best pilot I can be. Besides, finances aren't my forte. Ship repairing isn't, either, otherwise I'd do the maintenance myself."

"If you're ever in my part of the galaxy, stop by my shop. I could use an apprentice."

She giggled. "Don't get me wrong. I've tried my hand at ship mechanics, I'm just terrible at it. Racing is the only thing I do well. What I really love!"

"Except you can't even do that because Kaizon won't let you."

"Yes." She picked up a hard fruit from the platter and rolled it around in her gloved palm. "Racing is all I know. The last few months have been the emptiest in my entire life. I'm … lost without it. You know?"

"Too well," Croft said with a bitter chuckle. "I'm a born tinkerer. Dismantled my dad's prized antique motorcycle down to its nuts and bolts when I was twelve, and, much to his surprise, managed to put it back together."

"You sound like a natural."

"So natural that it drives Maria nuts. More than once she's had to drag me out of the garage to some social engagement or other. I don't complain, but …"

"You'd rather be in the garage. Just like I'd rather be pushing maximum gees through an asteroid field than shuttling businessmen on ice mining surveys." She tossed the hard fruit back onto the plate, where it landed with a solid *thunk.* "I feel like I'm being punished. I only wish Kaizon would tell me why."

"Have you asked him?"

"Well … not in so many words. He has a lot on his mind these days. He used to love watching me race, but now all he thinks about is his water trading business and the next big opportunity."

"Like Maria."

"Probably. Is she successful?"

"I'd say. She's always gushing about how she secured trade rights with such and such, bought a new transport, and all the profits they generate. It makes her giddy." Croft sighed. "It's the only time she smiles."

"At least something makes her happy, right?"

"Yeah."

I just wish that something were me.

Croft rubbed his face and forced a smile. "So, if you love racing so much, why not sign on with another team?"

"Kaizon holds my contract, so to speak." She pulled her knees up to her chest. "It's … complicated."

Back off, in other words.

Croft wouldn't make that mistake again. He picked up the fruit she had discarded. In the dim light, he couldn't discern its color, but it smelled musty and slightly acrid, like aged mustard.

Why not? I didn't fly across the galaxy to balk at new experiences.

Human teeth, apparently, weren't as sharp or sturdy as krurgik teeth. Croft managed to scrape a thin layer of pulp from its tough surface, then set it in his lap. The mysterious fruit tasted like it smelled, which wasn't bad, but not good enough to risk a trip to the dentist.

"Oh, I'm sorry," she said. "I only researched human digestive tracts, not their oral physiology. Allip fruit is soft in the center. Allow me."

She took the teeth-scraped fruit from him and popped it beneath her hood, where he imagined her mouth would be. A loud *crunch* raised the hair on his neck and made his own teeth ache in sympathy. It emerged in two halves, which she presented in a gloved hand.

"Better?"

"Um … sure."

Not wanting to be rude, Croft surreptitiously examined it for slobber, but found none except his own where his lips had brushed on his first attempt. Krurgik evidently had different hygiene etiquette than humans. The inside of the allip fruit was pink and fleshy, and, in stark contrast to its outside, smelled like peppermint. Fortunately, it tasted like it smelled, although its gritty texture reminded Croft of toothpaste.

"Not bad. What's in the jug, if I may ask?"

"The krurgik call it *grrachnak*. It's a beverage harvested from tall underwater plants, similar to Earthen trees."

"You know about trees?"

She bowed her head. "I've been researching your planet since our first communication after you exited the skipstream. Your society is fascinating. So much freer than Gralinov."

"Your home planet?"

"Kaizon's home."

"Where are you from, then?"

She drummed her fingers on her robe. "I'm … from Sothaostea, originally."

"Sothaostea? They produce some of the finest ships in the galaxy! A pain to service, but you can't beat the performance. I guess that explains why you're so into racing. Was this ship made there?"

"It was." Her voice dropped to a bashful whisper. "Do you like it?"

Croft chuckled. "Hard to say. The light level is a bit low for human eyes. Truth be told, I can barely see."

"Oh, I'm so sorry! Is this better?"

The interior brightened to a chill twilight, still dark, but at least now Croft could pick out details of his surroundings.

To a mechanic like himself, the sight hit him like a punch to the gut. Damage marked the surrounding consoles with missing buttons, cracked screens, and malfunctioning lights. The nearest seat sported a large rip in the fabric, its material food-stained from numerous spills.

His hands itched.

Croft could fix it. Half the repairs he could perform with the tools and supplies on *Majestic*. The rest would require a little time in a machine shop to fabricate the parts. Combined with a few touch-ups of the right color paint, he could have this ship looking like new in no time.

"It's beautiful," Croft said dreamily. He could already envision the finished work.

"You really think so?"

"Absolutely. Don't get me wrong; it could stand a few repairs, but the design is brilliant."

She bounced in her seat and clapped her hands. "Would you like to sit in the pilot's chair?"

"Won't Kaizon be upset?"

"Absolutely. But *I* want you to sit in it. Please! Will you?"

"Um ... sure."

Even if he hadn't wanted to — which he did — Croft could hardly refuse such a plea, especially from the woman who'd saved his life. He climbed the last few meters to the front of the cockpit. A white protective sphere encased the pilot's chair. Closer examination showed that the chair, too, had freedom of movement inside the sphere, providing additional dampening for high-g maneuvers.

As soon as Croft settled in, a console slid in front of him, complete with a flight stick, pedals, and readouts in a language he couldn't hope to decipher. The seat hugged him like a dream, actively molding itself to the contours of his body.

"Everything okay?" she said from behind him.

"Incredible. If *Majestic* had seats like these, I'd take her out more often."

"G-glad to hear. Just be careful with the — *unh!*"

Croft jerked his hand away from the flight stick, which he had grabbed, and climbed out so he could peer down. "Are you okay?"

"Fine. Fine! I just ... tripped. Be gentle with the controls, please. They're, um, d-delicate."

"Okay."

Delicate flight controls. Huh.

Left to him, that would be the first thing Croft fixed.

He started to settle back into the chair when a gleaming metallic cable caught his eye that he hadn't seen when he'd been down with her. It ran out from under her robe, and appeared to be fastened to the wall.

Croft's blood boiled. This time, he couldn't hold his tongue, manners or no.

"Are you *shackled?*"

She glanced behind her, then hastily covered the cable with the excess hem of her robe.

"Is that how Kaizon keeps you here? By chaining you to the damned *ship?*"

"No! It ..." Her shoulders drooped. She shook her head, but remained silent.

Croft scrambled out of the chair, down the ladder, and resumed his seat beside her. "Whatever it is, you can tell me. Please."

"I hardly know you," she said softly.

Croft rubbed his hands down his face and bottled a scream. The idea of her being chained like some sort of beast made him angrier than he could ever recall.

He didn't care about Earthen versus Gralinovian customs. Incarcerating an innocent person against their will was wrong. Period.

Unless ...

Is she a criminal?

Perhaps she was serving some strange Gralinovian sentence for crimes against Kaizon. Maybe she'd attempted to steal his ship. Cheated at cards, or at the races.

Or something much, much worse.

Croft closed his eyes and took a deep breath. "What ifs" were getting the better of him. He needed facts. Until he had them, he would have to trust his instincts. And his instincts told him she was no criminal.

Not the dangerous sort, at least.

It would, however, explain her reluctance to discuss it, and why she'd claimed she had no right to invite him aboard.

Croft bowed his head, unable to meet her eyes — not that he could see them under her hood anyway.

"I ... I should go," he said. "I've imposed enough on your hospitality."

She jerked upright, raised her hand as if to object, but sagged back upon herself. "I understand. Thank you for coming."

"And thank you for the allip fruit. It was … an experience, for sure." Croft stood to leave, but his eye lingered on the platter. "May I take one with me?"

She held it out to him. Croft picked a whole fruit and slipped it into his pocket.

"Goodbye, Croft."

Her voice held such loneliness — such a lack of hope and happiness — that Croft almost lost his resolve. Maria and Kaizon would likely be gone for a while longer. He could stay and keep her company. It would only be fair.

Except there was too much he didn't know. If his criminal theory proved true, Croft might be breaking Gralinovian law just by speaking with her, which could get them both in trouble.

Still, he couldn't possibly leave her feeling so down.

"Oh, I almost forgot. I brought that present I mentioned."

She perked up. "You did?"

"Aye." Croft dug the coins out of his pocket, this time looking for one in particular.

Aha!

He held it out. Even in the dim twilight, twin molten tracks gleamed across its surface, bright against the rest of its dull, worn face.

She gave a short, sad laugh. "You said it wouldn't be a coin."

"It isn't." He reverently placed it in her gloved hand. "It's an electric circuit that won the 271st Grand Yereleth Asteroid Run six Earth years ago."

"But … it *looks* like a coin."

"Because it was, once upon a time." Croft sat back down and leaned close to her. "I started my career as a pit mechanic for Harv Bender."

She gasped. "Harv Bender? Eight-time champion of the G.Y.A.R? *Twelve*-time winner of the Reithoin Ring Slalom? Holder of the galactic micro black-hole rally speed record?"

"The same," Croft said, laughing.

She grabbed his hand. "Please! Can you introduce me? I'd give anything to meet him. Anything!"

"If we're ever together at one of his races, I could probably arrange something."

"Done! I'm sure I can talk Kaizon into it. He's a fan, too." Her hood turned back to the coin. "So how did this win the race?"

"A secondary power coupling blew during the last lap. It was my fault, really. Pre-race electrical diagnostics were my responsibility. I should have caught the faulty connector and fixed it before he hit the course."

"Don't blame yourself. I'm sure you did everything you could."

"Thanks," Croft said. "Be that as it may, replacing the coupling would have taken too much time, and cost Harv the race. My welding equipment also would have taken too long to setup. I only needed to bridge the voltage gap long enough for him to complete one more lap. So I grabbed the nearest metal object — that coin — slapped it on top, triggered a surge of electricity through the system to weld it in place, and sent him on his way. Harv finished the race three-tenths of a second ahead of the next runner up."

"That's incredible! And how inventive. Very quick thinking."

"I was lucky the coin didn't melt and short-circuit the entire engine. I was so embarrassed that I removed it as soon as Harv pulled in from his victory lap so no one else would discover the danger I'd put him in."

"You took a risk. It paid off. End of story."

"Yes it did." Croft closed her fingers around the coin and held her hand tight. "And if you decide you're ready to take a risk while we're both at the Truck Stop, you know how to reach me. Take care."

Croft patted her hand, then climbed down the ladder toward the airlock.

The shackled woman, whose name and appearance were still a mystery, watched him go in silence.

7

REQUEST

CROFT HAD JUST PULLED HIS PAJAMAS ON when his data pad chimed with an incoming message. His heart leaped with excitement. It had to be either Maria or the chained woman on Kaizon's ship — which, in his mind, was a no-lose situation.

The message turned out to be from Maria.

DOCKING NOW, WILL SEE YOU SOON. I HAVE GOOD NEWS. CAN'T WAIT TO TELL YOU.

Croft sat on the bed and considered her message — and his reply.

LOOKING FORWARD TO IT. I HAVE NEWS, TOO. GETTING READY FOR BED, BUT I'LL WAIT UP FOR YOU.

He set his data pad aside and relaxed onto the pillow. Compared to the pilot's chair on Kaizon's ship, the station bed felt like lying on granite. He'd never been as comfortable as he had in that chair — so *right,* as if it had been made just for him. Now that he'd had a taste, he couldn't get it out of his mind.

Nor could he forget the woman chained to the wall.

Croft sighed. How much should he tell Maria? The chained woman had made clear that she'd broken the rules by having him aboard. If Maria knew, she might inform Kaizon and put her in even more trouble.

But, by the great cosmos, he had to tell someone or he might burst.

An airy chime sounded from the door, which Croft guessed was the doorbell.

"Good evening, Mr. Winder," a small bot said when Croft opened the door. It proffered a covered silver tray from one of its many hands. "I have brought the meal you ordered. May I come in and set a place for you?"

"But I didn't order a meal." Room service cost more limbs than Croft's already hurting bank account could afford.

"The order may have been placed by someone else. Ms. Gobber, perhaps? Either way, any mistake in delivery will be on the house, so you may as well enjoy the meal."

"Oh. Well, when you put it that way ..." Croft gestured for the bot to enter, where it rolled to a small table in the corner.

The idea that Maria may have ordered a meal for him made Croft giddy. It would be thoughtfulness on a level she hadn't shown since their early days of dating.

Maybe this getaway isn't a complete disaster after all.

The little bot pulled a seat out for him, which Croft accepted. The bot pulled the silver cover off, releasing a billowing cloud of steam, along with a host of savory smells that made Croft's mouth water. Apparently, he was hungry after all.

"Thank you ...?"

"Nisax. At your service, Mr. Winder." The little bot gave a squeaky bow that put Croft's teeth on edge.

"Oh no, that will never do. Wait right there, Nisax."

"But your meal —"

"Will be fine for a few minutes, especially if you cover it back up." Without waiting for consent, Croft grabbed his bag of tools and set to finding the offensive sound.

As with the medical robot, Nisax's troubles went well beyond a squeak. Twenty minutes of tweaking, lubricating, and a few spot welds had the little bot in much better condition. It still needed work, but if Croft tried to fix everything, he'd still be tinkering when Maria arrived, which would *not* go over well.

Nisax flexed its many arms without a squeak to be heard, then spun in a happy circle.

"Thank you, Mr. Winder! I have not been this close to fully operational since the day I arrived at this station. Please, wash yourself and sit. I shall remain here to ensure your meal is as enjoyable as possible."

And it was. Croft didn't recognize a single item on his plate, but he didn't care. Each bite burst with sinful deliciousness. When not a scrap remained on his plate, guilt struck him that he hadn't saved even a bite for Maria. He consoled himself by vowing he would order another plate for her if she wanted.

"And now, dessert." Nisax produced a small silver tray seemingly from nowhere and placed it on the table.

After such a tasty meal, Croft could hardly wait. He hovered in anticipation.

Instead of a chocolate masterpiece, as he'd expected, a long, thin electronic device lay across the plate, one Croft didn't recognize.

"I shall allow you to enjoy the rest of your meal in peace, Mr. Winder." Nisax rolled away, but paused at the door. "By the way, an unexpected failure with the station's docking system has delayed Ms. Gobber. She and Mr. Terazod are in no danger, but they will be unable to depart *Majestic* for another thirty minutes at least. Good night."

Croft sat back. Tired or not, he'd been looking forward to seeing Maria. The delay also meant she would be with Kaizon for that much longer.

He examined the stick-like device. A single button protruded from its stem. He pressed it.

"Surprise," the chained mystery woman said weakly from the device. "I hope this isn't a bad time."

"Apparently not." Croft suddenly suspected that Maria's unexpected docking failure was more than just happenstance. "Look, I really do appreciate you calling, but —"

"You told me to reach out when I'm ready to take a risk. I am."

"But ... sabotaging the station's docking systems? Isn't that a little extreme?"

"What's wrong with the docking systems?"

Croft blinked. "That ... wasn't you?"

"I don't see how it could be. The station's security is iron-clad. Even if it wasn't, I'm no hacker. Are Maria and Kaizon all right?"

"From what I hear. Look, if it wasn't you, then ... how do you keep getting these modules and such to me?"

"Same way you keep receiving special service from the staff. Being nice pays." She took a deep breath. "I ... I have a favor to ask, and it's going to sound strange."

"If it's within my power to give, name it."

"That's exactly what I want. Croft, I haven't given you my name yet because I ... I don't have one. It's part of the terms of my, um ... service. Property can't be named. At least, not as far as Kaizon is concerned. Naming myself is expressly forbidden.

"But *you* can. My service puts no stipulations on what other people choose to do or call me. Technically, I'm not even allowed to ask you to name me, so ... so I'll leave it at that."

"You want *me* to name you? But I hardly know you."

"You know me better than you think. Better than Kaizon. Better than anyone I've ever met. If anyone is qualified to name me, it's you."

Croft rubbed his face. "Can I say how incredibly odd this feels? And intimidating. It's one thing to name a newborn whose personality has yet to form, but a full-grown adult ..."

"I ... Well, you don't have to, of course. And if you don't, I'll ... I'll understand."

The crushing despair in her voice nearly broke Croft in half. Why was he balking, anyway? He'd named ships before, and had put much thought into each one. Was naming a person any different?

Croft ran through what he knew of her in his mind: her humor, her wit, her insecurity, her kindness, her bravery ...

"Blossom."

The communicator stayed quiet for so long that, for a minute, Croft thought the connection had dropped.

"Why that name?" she said eventually, her voice rough with emotion.

"Because that's what you are: a bud on a gigantic tree — small, alone, but on your way to becoming the most glorious flower the galaxy has ever seen."

Silence.

"Are you still there?"

"I ... I have to go," she said, barely choking out the words.

The connection light turned off.

Croft was still staring at the inactive communication stick when Maria returned, snapping him out of his brain-locked stupor inflicted by the strange, emotional conversation.

She tossed her jacket on the bed, then flopped onto her back beside it. "Croft, you won't believe what just happened!"

Ditto.

"You mean the docking system issues?"

"You heard? Well, I shouldn't be surprised. You probably know every mechanic and droid on the entire station by now." Sadly, Maria didn't sound happy about that. "Anyhow, you'll never guess what Kaizon and I discussed!"

"A water trading deal?"

"Not just any deal. An alliance between his company and mine." Maria sat up, eyes sparkling to match her giant grin. "I had no idea when you booked our vacation that this decrepit Truck Stop parked by the mother of all black holes would be such a gold mine of opportunity."

"So you're trading gold now, too?"

She threw her jacket at him and frowned. "Figure of speech, Croft! I'm talking *water.* All stations need it, sure, but *this* station is the only stop for thousands of light years in any direction. It's poised to become *the* galactic trading center — like Venice in the Middle Ages. And, since it's only recently come into service, exclusive water trading rights have not yet been established." Maria crossed her arms. Her teeth flashed a predatory smile. "Kaizon and I aim to change that."

"Maria, I-I know how excited you are about this, but —"

"But *you* aren't."

Anger and frustration flared across her face, wrinkling her black eyebrows in a steep V. She took a deep breath, which seemed to relax her, then sat across from him at the table.

"Croft, securing this deal could be my big break. *Our* big break. The profit opportunities are insane. In a few years, we could vacation anywhere you want, as often as you want. You could open garages all across the cosmos. Become the biggest ship mechanic chain in the galaxy! Doesn't that make you happy?"

Not nearly as happy as it makes you, Croft thought sadly, but he couldn't say it aloud. The glint in her eye was back. Telling her the truth would snuff it out like fire in a vacuum. He loved her excitement, her enthusiasm — even if the topic didn't thrill him personally.

Still, there was one issue he couldn't ignore.

"Maria, I *am* happy for you, as always. I just wonder if you couldn't find another partner."

"Happy for *us*." Maria said it so softly that Croft almost missed it. She fixed her raptor gaze on him and continued more sternly. "What's wrong with Kaizon? I thought you got along peachily with everybody."

"It's not that we don't get along, though I'm a little surprised that you and he get along so well."

"What's that supposed to mean? I *am* capable of getting along with others, you know!"

"Whoa! That isn't what I meant at all. Kaizon just comes across as, ah ... sexist, to put it mildly, and I know how that upsets you."

"I can handle sexist assholes, Croft. I've been doing it all my life. True, I didn't expect it from a red-skinned dog-alien, but I put him in his place after his second sentence. Guess how he took it?"

"Not a clue."

"He laughed. And then he *thanked* me! Said he wished krurgik women would speak up for themselves like I did. We got along great after that, even though I had to slap his wrist a few more times for talking down to me." Maria folded her hands and leaned forward. "What I'm saying, Croft, is that I don't need your protection from, or approval for, people I choose to do business with."

Croft could only stare, taken aback by the harsh tone he'd become accustomed to hearing in her business deals, but never against himself. He rallied with a shake of his head. Maria had to know.

"Did Kaizon tell you about the woman chained in his ship?"

Maria went ashen. "The what?"

Against his better judgment, Croft filled her in on the details, beginning with Blossom's crying when they'd first disembarked, and ending with their conversation just before Maria had returned, where Blossom had practically begged Croft for the basic right of having a name.

As soon as he finished, Maria sagged into her chair. Moist brown eyes found his. "You ... were with another woman?"

Croft tried to speak, but couldn't. How Maria could have taken only *that* away from everything he'd just told her was so incomprehensible that he didn't even know how to respond. So he simply sat there, staring at her with his mouth open, trying to figure out where he'd gone wrong, and how to fix it.

Then she jumped him, wielding passionate kisses as if they were weapons. She stripped his clothes and her own as fast as her shaking fingers could move, leaving Croft even more confused and unsettled than if she'd simply screamed at him.

•　　　•　　　•

Maria lay in Croft's arms, tense despite their fervid and unexpected romp.

Nothing felt right. Not her taking to Kaizon. Not her reaction to Croft's revelation about Blossom chained inside Kaizon's ship. And certainly not this, whatever "this" had been.

Although, when Croft thought back, Maria had reacted this way before. She'd done it once after a party, when a woman his age had asked him to dance. Maria had practically dragged him upstairs, locked them inside a random guest room, and attacked him with carnal intent. It hadn't been sweet or romantic, just pure aggression, as if she were claiming him, marking Croft as her own regardless of his wishes.

It's almost as if she's ...

"Jealous," Croft said aloud. "You're jealous of Blossom. Is that what this is about?"

Maria stiffened. Her teeth ground together, sending unpleasant vibrations through his ribs. "That's ridiculous, Croft. Why would I be jealous of a woman chained to a ship?"

"Then please explain why you just ravaged me like a madwoman. It isn't like you at all."

Maria looked up at him. "Are you seriously complaining?"

"Only because it felt ... forced. Desperate. You didn't want me, Maria. You were hiding from something else. What?"

Growling, she pounded his chest, then sprang out of bed. The Habitat Ring's low gravity flung her farther than she'd evidently expected. Maria stumbled with a few choice curses, then began pacing the small room.

"It … it's what you always do, Croft! No matter where we go, people are drawn to you like a magnet in ferrous asteroid dust. Men, women, even *bots* can't get enough of you. Ever!" Maria turned to him with wild eyes and gripped her hair with both hands. "Do you have any idea how difficult that is to compete with? Especially for someone like me who … who …"

"Who *what?*"

"Who's insecure! Socially awkward! Who's never made friends easily, and even when I do, I can't seem to keep them for long." She plonked down at the table and put her face in her hands. "Every time I see you with another woman I … I freak out, wondering if this will be the person you finally leave me for. And this Blossom lady! She's right up your alley. Kind, in distress, *and* on a ship in need of repair." She gave a bitter laugh. "If you only knew the number of times I almost took a crowbar to *Majestic* just to give you something to fix so you'd stick around.

"But it isn't enough. You need someone to rescue, someone you can fix like one of your machines. And I don't do the whole 'damsel in distress' thing very well. It isn't in my nature." Maria's voice dropped to a whisper. "And I'm deathly afraid that's why I'm going to lose you, like I've lost everyone else."

Croft closed his eyes. If any more bombshells dropped on him tonight, his head would surely explode.

"For the record," he said eventually, "I booked this vacation because I thought I was going to lose *you*."

"Why would you ever think something so stupid?"

"Because your head is always in that business of yours. It's like nothing else matters. Including me."

Maria's jaw dropped as if he'd just told her the galaxy's core were actually made of monkeys. "I push the business *because* of you! I'm not cuddly or helpless, but I have a nose for deals, and the fortitude to be successful. If I can't fill your other needs, I can at least make sure you're comfortable, and provide for you like a responsible spouse should."

"A … a spouse?"

Maria's hands flew to her mouth. She stared at him, eyes teary and wide, shaking her head.

Before Croft could utter a word, she grabbed a robe and fled from the room.

8

MARIA

MARIA STUMBLED THROUGH the Habitat Ring toward the spoke. The rough metal floor bit her tender, bare feet with every step, but she was too upset to care. Months of agonizing over how she would propose to Croft had just imploded in one, colossal blunder. Maria wasn't romantic by nature — which she had just proven beyond any shadow of a doubt.

She entered the elevator, tightened her fluffy white robe around her, and pressed the button for the Docking Ring.

Docking Ring?

Why would she go there? The bars were on the Main Ring.

But Maria already knew the answer.

Blossom.

Kaizon had returned to his room after they'd departed *Majestic*, which gave Maria unfettered access to the woman Croft had broken the law to speak with — an act Maria intended to repeat.

There was a problem, of course. Maria wasn't Croft. She didn't have an army of fan-bots to help her gain access to Kaizon's ship.

Or do I?

Maria pushed the button for the Main Ring and tapped her foot, waiting for the doors to open.

The Truck Stop bustled with activity, as always. Maria felt ridiculous stepping into the throng wearing nothing but her robe, but the feeling quickly passed. Several alien species wore no clothes at all, and bots wouldn't care one way or the other. Besides, her robe was thicker than three jumpsuits combined, and plenty warm.

"Excuse me," Maria said, flagging down a squat robot carrying a piece of luggage on each of its many arms.

"Ms. Gobber." The bot dipped its binocular eyes in imitation of a bow. "It is a pleasure to meet you. How are you and Mr. Winder enjoying your stay?"

"It's been an experience." Maria cleared her throat. "Listen, I need a favor."

"I shall do my best to fulfill your needs. What do you require?"

"Access to a ship that isn't mine."

"I am afraid I cannot comply, Ms. Gobber. That is against station regulations, and would incur punishment on us both." The bot studied her for a moment. "Speaking hypothetically, to which ship do you need access?"

"Kaizon Terazod's. I need to speak with someone on board."
Before I go out of my mind.

"I see. Well, as I stated, I cannot help. But if you wait here, a service robot will be along momentarily with a refreshment that may ease your worries."

"I don't need a drink, I need access to that ship! *Please!*"

"Friends of Mr. Winder are friends of mine, Ms. Gobber. Have a pleasant night, and please relay that Bult gives him kindest regards."

The little bot dipped its binocular eyes again and toddled off.

Maria plopped onto a bench, gritting her teeth. That had, unfortunately, gone as well as most of her attempts at social persuasion.
Friends of Mr. Winder are friends of mine.

What had Bult even meant? Was it referring to Maria? Or to Blossom?

Maria's social skills were so dull that she couldn't even fence with a sodding luggage bot. What hope did she have of keeping the most empathetic man she'd ever met? Let alone marrying him?

Despair pulled her shoulders down as if the station's rotation speed had doubled.

She shook herself and straightened. Giving up was *not* how she'd built a thriving water trading business from scratch. And it certainly wasn't how she would win Croft back.

No, Maria needed to learn more about her competition.

One person could get her on that ship for sure — Kaizon — and it was high time she spoke with him.

"Ms. Gobber, glad I ran into you."

Maria spun to find the security officer who'd met them at the dock smiling at her. Robbins, if she remembered.

"I was just about to send you our diagnostic report of your ship's autopilot system," Robbins said. "But, since you're already here, I might as well deliver it in person. The system itself, you'll be happy to know, works great."

"Then why did it spit us out of the skipstream on a collision course with the station!"

"As far as we can tell, an intense electromagnetic pulse knocked it out during skipstream."

"Is that normal?"

"Not remotely. Our engineers tell me that the skipstream attenuates electromagnetic radiation. To have knocked out your autopilot, the pulse would need to have been really close." Robbins' eyes narrowed. "And probably intentional."

"Intentional? Like an EM bomb or something?"

"Can't say for sure without more information. Don't worry, though. The incident is under active investigation."

"Active how?"

"I shouldn't say. If the incident was an attack, then the less the responsible party knows about the investigation, the better."

"Including me," Maria said, feeling her defensive hackles rise.

"Yep. Not that you're a suspect right now, Ms. Gobber, but it never hurts to be cautious. Anyway, the full diagnostic report will be in your inbox shortly. Reach out to me directly if you have any questions."

"Thank you, I will."

Maria held her breath, certain that Bult had turned her in for conspiring to infiltrate a ship, but Robbins simply tipped his head and turned to leave.

She exhaled in a *whoosh.* Maybe Bult considered her a friend, after all.

Robbins stopped not a step away.

Damn, here it comes.

Maria braced for confrontation, but the officer wasn't focused on her. Across the ring, the shady treasure hunters they'd run into near the docking ramp were all smiles with a man in gray station uniform. Sturm joked loudly, while Pitts occasionally touched the uniformed man in an overly affectionate way that made Maria pull her robe tighter. Even she could tell they were trying to butter him up for something.

"Speaking of suspects," Robbins said under his breath.

"Who are they talking to?" It was none of Maria's business, but she couldn't help asking.

"A Space Traffic Controller."

"Odd. What could they want?"

"That's what I need to find out. Sorry, Ms. Gobber, would you excuse me?"

"Of course."

Maria breathed a sigh of relief when Robbins headed toward the trio. She'd dodged yet another legal meteor strike.

"Refreshments," a mechanical voice said behind her. "Refreshments. Refreshments."

She turned and nearly tripped over a knee-high machine more resembling a cooler than a robot.

"No, thank you."

Maria started for the elevator. She had a mission. She dreaded the conversation with Kaizon, but it couldn't be helped. She *had* to meet Blossom.

"Refreshments. Refreshments." The cooler bot zipped in front of her, blocking her path. "Refreshments."

"Oh, all right! I'll take an Orion Red. Or if you don't have that, gin on the rocks." Maria hated mixing alcohol and business, but the way this night was shaping up, a drink didn't sound terrible.

The little bot whirred. Seconds later, a glass with red liquid and an abnormally large swizzle stick rose up through a small hole. Maria accepted the drink and reached for her data pad to pay, only to remember she'd left it in her room, along with her shoes and the rest of her clothes.

"Sorry, I don't have my ..."

Maria fell silent when the cooler bot zipped away.

Oh well. I won't complain about a free drink.

She took a sip.

Not bad.

The swizzle stick was one of the strangest she'd seen; a button sat smack dab in the middle of it.

A powered swizzle, maybe?

Fancier hotels sometimes gave them as gimmicks, although Truck Stop didn't strike her as one of those. Curious, she pressed the button.

"Croft?" a woman's voice said.

Maria almost dropped her drink. The voice had come from the swizzle stick.

"No, this is Maria Gobber — Croft's *girlfriend*. To whom am I speaking?" The question was rhetorical, since Maria had a fairly good idea already.

"Oh no! I-is Kaizon with you?"

"He isn't, and neither is Croft. It's just you and me."

Blossom gulped. "You won't tell Kaizon about me going around his little communication ban, will you?"

"No. In fact, I'd like to come aboard and speak with you. In private."

"Two unauthorized visitors in one day? Kaizon will have a conniption if he finds out."

"Then you'd better not tell him, because I certainly won't."

"Oh ... okay. Come down to the hatch and I'll read you the access code."

Maria was sprinting for the elevator before Blossom had finished her sentence.

•   •   •

By the time Maria had climbed up the last few steps to the cockpit of Kaizon's ship, her blood was boiling. She hated this woman she'd never met for simply existing — for luring Croft away with an innocence and vulnerability that Maria would never possess.

Maria didn't bow to competition. She crushed it.

Just like she would crush Blossom.

The target of her angst stood on the rear wall of the cockpit, completely enshrouded in a dark robe that hid even her face.

"Welcome," Blossom said, surprisingly in English. "How can I help you?"

Her voice was light. Airy. Pleasant. Maria hated her all the more.

"Croft told me so much about you," Maria said. "I just wanted to chat for a minute to see what captivated him so."

"He's captivated? With *me?*" Blossom twirled her robe like a bashful girl at prom night. "I can't imagine why. I'm a terrible host who nearly broke his teeth on an allip fruit. And I bug him constantly."

"Mm." Maria locked her jaw to keep from shouting. The woman radiated sweetness like a cotton candy supernova. Worst of all, it seemed genuine.

Maria could never compete with that.

Never.

She turned away, pretending to examine her surroundings while she considered her next move.

Why had she come here? What had she hoped to accomplish, apart from torturing herself?

The answer came when she spied a nearby tool cabinet fastened to the wall — and, through its glass door, a wrench the size of her forearm.

"Ms. Gobber? Are you a mechanic, too?"

Maria looked down. She didn't remember opening the cabinet, but there the wrench sat in her white-knuckled grip.

"No," she said, deathly soft. "I don't fix things. I only break them. That's all I ever seem to do, no matter how hard I try."

Maria advanced. The wrench felt heavy in her hand. Plenty heavy enough.

"Oh! I know what you mean." Blossom collapsed into a chair and hung her head. "That's all I seem to do, too."

"Mm, break things."

Cold iron settled into Maria's stomach, as if she and the wrench were one. She stopped within arm's reach of the mysterious woman, towering over her frail, shrouded form.

"Like relationships?"

Maria's arm raised of its own accord. The solid tool loomed over Blossom's bowed head like a steel thundercloud.

"Exactly like that," Blossom said into her hands. "I've sacrificed so much to try to make Kaizon happy. But everything I do implodes, and he ends up being even more upset with me, making us both miserable."

"Miserable."

The word echoed in Maria's empty chest.

Yes, she was miserable. Everything she did to bring Croft closer only seemed to push him away. The harder she tried, the greater the rift became. Maria was flailing in open vacuum without a spacesuit, holding her breath and grasping at anything that might pull her back to safety. But every desperate swipe found only empty space.

The wrench slipped from her limp fingers.

Maria screamed when she realized it was on a collision course with Blossom's head.

She fumbled to catch it. Her finger jammed against its solid metal handle, making her see stars, but her fingers failed to close around it. To her horror, the wrench struck the back of Blossom's hood with a loud, metallic *clang!*

"Oh my stars! Blossom, I'm so sorry! Are you all ..."

Wait a minute, it clanged?

Blossom rubbed the back of her head. "What happened?"

She didn't even sound injured. Maria grabbed the back of her hood, whipped it back ...

... and gasped.

She collapsed to her knees, staring in a confused, if relieved, daze at the woman who had captivated her would-be fiancée.

Well, this certainly explains things.

9

TRUTH

CROFT CAUGHT A WHIFF of the same exotic spices he'd smelled on Kaizon's ship. He looked up from his dingy bar booth to find a familiar set of wicked sharp teeth grinning at him.

"Croft! You look like the" — his translator blanked —"ate your sandwich. Where's Maria?"

With you, I thought.

Clearly, he'd been wrong.

"Doing her own thing," Croft said instead, keeping as close to the truth as he dared.

Kaizon barked a laugh. "Probably does that whether you like it or not. She's a feisty thing, but I like it." He plopped into the booth seat across from Croft and drummed his sharp black talons on the table. "So, if you didn't call me here about business, then this must be about drinking. At least, I hope it is."

It is now.

Croft flagged a serving bot. It and the bot next to it sped over in a whir of spinning wheels. They clanked together at the edge of the table, shoulder to shoulder. One shoved the other, who shoved back.

"Mr. Winder hailed *me*," the first one said, whom Croft had actually hailed.

The other shook its domed head. "He clearly hailed *me*. Kindly return to your duties, and I shall see to Mr. Winder's needs."

"I cannot let your error go unremedied." Its cylindrical body turned fully toward the second bot. In a human-like gesture, it planted one spindly metal arm just above its motor housing, where a person's hip might be. "Mr. Winder desires my services, and that is precisely what he shall receive."

"Mr. Winder desires a bot with functional optics, which yours evidently are not, because if they were —"

Croft cleared his throat. "Gentlemen — er, gentlebots, please. We're going to order drinks *and* food. Perhaps you can divide the responsibilities between you?"

Although neither of their faces were capable of displaying emotion, Croft swore he saw animosity in their glowing eyes when they stared at each other in chilly silence.

They eventually turned as one to him and bowed.

"We apologize," they said at the same time.

"Allow us to make amends," the first bot said.

"We will return shortly to take your orders," the second bot said.

Then they both wheeled away.

Kaizon wiped his hands down his face. "Yap, yap, yap. Holy Mother Universe, the tin cans on this station are the worst I've ever seen! They didn't even take our orders. We'll be lucky if they don't bring us water from the urinals." He shook his maned head. "Suddenly, I ain't that thirsty."

"What do you have against robots?" Croft hadn't meant to sound accusatory, but Kaizon's lofty tone boiled it out of him. "They're doing their best, just like the rest of us."

"Us? *Us?* Croft, they ain't like us! Nothing but gears for brains. Built for purposes they seem to screw up half the time anyway. Like your autopilot, am I right? It had one freakin' job: don't hit anything! And it nearly splattered you and Maria against the station's hull." Kaizon's gaze dropped to the table. His voice softened. "More trouble than they're worth, I tell ya, or I'm a toothless pup."

"Speaking of Maria ..." Croft loosened his collar, unsure how to broach the subject. The "spouse" bombshell Maria had dropped before fleeing their hotel room had left him with two certainties: she needed space to cool off, and, in contradiction, Croft *had* to know how she was doing.

"Oh, yeah," Kaizon said, snapping out of his funk. His toothy grin reappeared. "You've got one helluva hotrod there! It's all I can do to keep up with her. How do you do it? I mean, you don't strike me as the alpha type. I'd think she'd chew you up and spit out the bloody parts after every conversation. Miracle there's anything left of you!"

"It feels like that sometimes," Croft said. They had their intense conversations, for sure. "But Maria treats me differently. Or, she did at first."

"What, she getting tired of you already?" Kaizon pounded Croft's shoulder in what had surely been meant as a friendly gesture, but knocked the wind out of him and clattered his teeth. "Don't jive with what I've heard, but you'd know best."

"She's talked about our relationship?"

"You kidding? She don't ever shut up about you. If I didn't know her better, I'd peg her as the clingy type." Kaizon shuddered.

Which she definitely isn't.

Croft shook his head to clear the strange revelations about the woman he thought he knew and returned to the reason he'd asked to meet Kaizon. "Have … have you seen her? Recently?"

"Not since we said goodbye after that docking delay." He gnashed his pointy teeth. "Stupid bots. One more example why they're nothing but trouble, the bunch of them."

Again, Croft sensed no heat behind his disparaging words, which seemed odd. But that paled next to Croft's incredible relief.

Maria hadn't fled to Kaizon. Better still, Croft didn't get the impression that Kaizon was interested in her, nor Maria in him. His romantic Truck Stop getaway plans may be salvageable yet.

One, big, gaping issue remained, however.

Blossom.

Unfortunately, she had made it clear that Kaizon would be furious if he learned she'd directly contacted Croft. He suspected Kaizon didn't even know she'd helped them by sending the nav program, especially since he hadn't yet brought it up. Croft would have to tread very carefully.

He still hadn't come up with a plan of attack by the time their robot servers returned. Each carried an exceptionally wide glass containing clear liquid in one hand, and a beaker of dark liquid in the other. They carefully set a wide glass each in front of Croft and Kaizon.

"To make amends for our inappropriate behavior," the first robot said.

"Please enjoy these special drinks," the second robot said. "On the house."

They poised their beakers high, then carefully tipped a single drop of dark liquid into each glass.

Crystals of various sizes formed at the snap of a finger, while the liquid itself turned from clear to a deep, heavenly blue in the blink of an eye. The largest crystals formed near the center, while other crystals floated in the void around it like celestial bodies.

Then, to Croft's amazement, the crystals began twinkling with their own light. Their density increased toward the center, culminating in a bright, glowing mass of swirling light.

It was a miniature universe in a glass.

Kaizon stared at his own drink, completely mesmerized. He poked a nail at the glass. "Tell me those ain't real stars."

"They are not," the first bot said. "The crystals were engineered by the Thaylonians at the request of their consulate exclusively to celebrate the five thousandth anniversary of their republic. No more were ever manufactured, making this a truly rare spectacle."

"We also confirmed that the ingredients are digestible by krurgiks and humans, so you need not worry," the second bot said. "We will return later for your food orders. In the meantime, please enjoy."

They bowed, then wheeled away, weaving through the crowd of gawkers that had formed around their table. From the corner of his eye, Croft swore he saw their servers fist-bump before they disappeared from view.

"Holy Mother Universe," Kaizon said, his eyes glued to the mesmerizing lights. "What do you reckon these drinks would go for on the open market?"

"Probably more than I make in a year."

Kaizon shook his head. "That tin can *did* say they were on the house, right?"

"Right."

Whether the proprietor of this restaurant knew what his employees had just given away was another matter. Croft suspected not, although he certainly wouldn't be the person to break the news.

Croft let them enjoy their twinkling galaxies for a few minutes, which also gave time for those who'd gathered to watch the spectacle to disperse, before breaking the silence to broach the second-biggest subject on his mind.

"So, it sounds like you've come to know Maria quite well in the brief time we've been here, and some of the troubles we're having, but you haven't told me much about *your* partner."

"Eh? What do you mean?" Kaizon sobered. "Oh, you're talking about what I said when we first met on the Docking Ring."

"Right. You mentioned that she's needy. In what way, may I ask?"

"It's complicated. You don't want to hear about that garbage."

"You heard my garbage, and have even helped Maria, in a way. Only fair that I return the favor, if I can."

Kaizon scratched his furry mane. "All right, you asked for it. But don't say I didn't warn you." He settled on his elbows and fixed his violet eyes on Croft. "For any of it to make sense, you gotta have some context first. And *I* need some of this drink." He picked it up with both hands and took a sip. "Mm, creation don't taste half bad."

Croft picked his own up. The twinkling crystals swirled little eddies, bringing the galaxy to life. It seemed a shame to consume such wonderful artwork. But if he didn't, he would always wonder, so he put it to his lips.

"Chemicals" was the only word Croft could think to describe the eclectic mix of flavors that assaulted his tongue. It was as if someone had picked a variety of lubricants and oils from his workbench back home, mixed them together, and called it a cocktail. Surprisingly, as Kaizon mentioned, it wasn't terrible.

Kaizon leaned back and draped an arm over his seat. "Ever heard of Cheybok Industries?"

"Cheybok ... No, can't say I have."

"Not surprised. They were a ship manufacturer who went out of business a long time ago." Kaizon frowned. "How long do you Earthens live, anyway?"

"Ninety years, give or take."

"Oh, wow, you ain't got much time, then. Gotta live large while you can, eh?"

"I suppose, though millions of years of evolution have given us plenty of time to be comfortable with what we're given."

"Fair enough," Kaizon said. "Anyway, so yeah, they went ker-*pow* probably not long after you popped into existence. Cheybok were famous for their performance ships. If you were serious about racing, you bought a Cheybok, or you lost. That's why I got mine."

"Oh, so your ship is a Cheybok?"

"Sure is. I ain't a racing pilot, mind you, but I love a good performance ship. Who doesn't?"

Croft couldn't argue, so he nodded. "Sounds like Cheybok had a great market position. Why did they go under?"

"Two reasons. First and foremost, they went a little too high-end for their own good. Servicing one is ridiculously pricey, and went insane after they tanked, but even the materials can cost more than a new mid-level ship."

"You must be doing pretty well for yourself, then."

Kaizon groaned. "I *was,* which was why I bought it. And since you can't really find them anymore, I thought I could hire a great pilot, win some races, and use the prize money to pay for repairs. All that, and I get a cool ride to cruise in during the off season. Sounds great, right?"

"Absolutely," Croft said. "If I were a betting man, I would have done the same."

"Yeah, well this betting man lost. Big time. Not the races, mind you. That Cheybok ate the competition for breakfast and shot it out the exhaust. Problem is, it's designed to ride hard. *Really* hard. Parts don't last long at all."

"Ouch."

"You said it. Damn thing broke down after the first race. I nearly had a heart attack when I saw the bill. Thought it was a fluke, so I tried another race. Same thing: won handedly, but it went straight back to the shop."

Kaizon took a long pull from his drink, then shook his head.

"Just 'cause I never learn, I thought I'd try one more to see if I could get two races out of it without breaking the bank. That's when it *really* broke. The repair bill was bigger than the prize money from any three races combined. I was so far in debt that I had to borrow from my business to pay it off."

"Wait … you *fixed* it?"

"Yeah, of course."

Croft blinked. "Well, I … I just thought that would have been your cue to cut your losses and sell it off, or even junk it. I mean, sounds like there's a reason there aren't any of them left."

"Oh, that ain't the only reason. And the irony is that I fixed it because of the second reason Cheybok went outta business."

"Which is?"

Kaizon wiped a hand down his face. He glanced at the bar, where their two servers were busy preparing for other patrons' meals. "Tell me, what's the difference between us and those tin cans? And don't go all philanthropic, equal rights on me, 'cause I know that's what you're thinking. I'm talking about their design."

Croft clamped his mouth shut. He had indeed been about to dig into Kaizon about equal rights for artificial lifeforms, but the clarification caught him off-guard.

"Well, apart from the obvious physical differences …" Croft considered for a moment. "Most service robots are, like you said earlier, built for a particular purpose. That's what sets them above hiring people for the same positions: they're more efficient."

"And?"

Croft took another sip of the chemical-tasting drink. The odd flavor was growing on him. "And … I guess they also like it. Or are programmed to like it."

"More than like it," Kaizon said. "They're programmed to *only* like the job they're designed for. Maintains job satisfaction for the 'can, and prevents the person who bought an autopilot from one day owning a wanna-be ballet dancer who hates piloting. Win-win all around."

"Cheybok didn't do that?"

"Not well enough. They were selling premium products to upper-class buyers with high-society needs. Their 'cans had to not only be the best pilots in the business, but they also had to be able to rub elbows with snobs and not embarrass their owners. That requires a lot more creative freedom than your average 'can, along with the ability to learn and grow in unexpected directions.

"And grow they did, with an emphasis on *unexpected.*" Kaizon took another swig and drained half his remaining glass in a single pull. "Damn if that don't hit the spot. Too bad we can't order any more of them."

"That would ruin their specialness, wouldn't it?"

"Too true! Ain't nearly as awesome when everyone else has access to the exact same thing." He wiped a napkin across his red lips, which came away blue. "Where was I?"

"Growing in unexpected directions," Croft said.

"Ah. So, as I understand, everything went hunky-dory for a while. The ships sold like icicles on a desert planet, the autopilots charmed the pants off people, and Cheybok made a fortune. But the rule they'd broken had been put in place for a reason, as they found out the hard way.

"The autopilots began learning. Expanding. Wanting things they'd never had — *couldn't* have — because they were part of the damned ship. Some went crazy and had to be decommissioned. Others became unstable and stopped working."

Kaizon tapped his glass, holding Croft's gaze. "What buried Cheybok, however, were the ones who decided to take themselves out of the picture in spectacular ways. And, in some very public cases, their owners with it."

"Holy Mother Universe," Croft said. He'd never uttered that phrase in his life, but in light of that horrifying revelation, it suddenly felt appropriate. "I can see why there aren't any more of them. Except *you* still have a Cheybok. How is it still functioning?"

"Mine was one of the last units ever produced. Even so, 'functioning' is a strong word. A few weeks ago, she did something that made me pull two full tufts of hair from my mane." Kaizon pointed at a pair of thin spots on the back of his neck. "See? Still hasn't grown back."

Croft barely noticed. Realization crushed the air from his lungs as if the galaxy's black hole were sitting on his chest. "Kaizon, y-you referred to your autopilot as 'she'?"

"Yeah. You asked about the girl driving me crazy, right? That's her. My ship's autopilot."

"Blossom," Croft said in a hollow voice.

"Huh?"

Croft put his hands in his head. "Blossom. That's what I named her, when I ... spoke to her. On your ship."

"You *what?*"

As much as Croft wanted to keep her confidence, the situation had just taken a dramatic turn. Withholding his conversations with Blossom could, if Kaizon's story was true, put both of them in danger. He couldn't possibly live with that on his conscience.

And so he told Kaizon everything, down to the last detail, followed by a sincere apology.

"Had I known," Croft said once he'd finished, feeling one meter tall, "I would never have ... I mean, I wouldn't ..."

Kaizon, who had listened to the entire story like a brick of tense muscle, collapsed onto the table, as if a puppet master had just cut his strings.

"No," Kaizon said, "you were just doing what any person with a shred of decency would have done if they saw another person in trouble. The problem goes back to that thing she did that made me tear out my hair."

"What did she do?"

Kaizon pressed his lips into a thin line. His pointy ears turned a deeper shade of red, and he looked away. "She ... had herself rewired. I didn't find out until after."

"Rewired how?" That didn't sound nearly as bad as Croft had been expecting.

Kaizon blew a long sigh. "Like I said, money's been tight. I was already at rock-bottom, trying to figure out how to keep afloat *and* keep her happy without decommissioning her."

"That's ... surprisingly noble."

Kaizon raised a furry eyebrow.

"I didn't mean it like that," Croft said, feeling his own cheeks color. "You're working your tail off for a robot — a ship, I guess — that every other owner had given up on, and seem genuinely concerned about her well-being. I don't know how many people would do the same."

"Do I look like a monster to you? *'course* I couldn't send her to the scrap without at least trying. She ain't a bad person, just … emotional." Kaizon screwed his lips in a sour expression. "I don't do well with feelings. Ain't got a clue how to deal with her now — *especially* after the rewiring."

"What exactly did she rewire?"

"Everything! Like I said, she got these feelings. She could tell the money situation bothered me, even though I never told her about it. She's touchy enough without putting that on her. Anyway, that turned out to be a mistake. She thought I was drifting away from her because she's a machine, or some nonsense. So she goes and has the *entire* interior of the ship rigged with touch sensors!"

Croft thought back to his experience on the ship — specifically, her gasp when he'd gripped the controls. "Oh wow, I … I think I know what you mean."

"Yeah. Ever since then, I can't touch a damned thing on my own ship without feeling like some sort of pervert! So I don't. Now, of course, she thinks I don't like her even more because I won't sit in the cockpit. Which, by the way, has the most touch sensors of anywhere."

Kaizon gripped his hair. For a moment, Croft thought he might lose another two tufts, but he sagged to the table.

"I'm out of my depth, Croft. If I didn't know better, I'd say she's in love with me, but I … man, I just can't. It ain't my thing. But I can't abandon her." He sagged farther, until his head lay flat on the table. "And I can't afford her, either. She can't race anymore because fixing her would cost my entire business. I can't even afford to have the wiring removed. And if I did, I'd probably just end up hurting her feelings.

"Worse, if she can't race — the one thing she was built for — I just know she's gonna go insane. Or shut down. Or …"

Or terminate herself, Croft finished for him.

Kaizon cracked a miserable eye and looked at him. "Bet you were expecting some typical relationship crap, huh? Didn't mean to dump all that on you, buddy, but I tell ya, if you've got any advice whatsoever, I'm all ears."

Sadly, Croft didn't. He could probably reverse the wiring job himself, maybe fix some of the superficial interior damage he'd spotted, but obtaining whatever materials were necessary to enable her to race again was beyond his meager financial abilities. And what would he do when she broke again? And again?

"Have you considered detaching her from the ship?"

Kaizon barked a bitter laugh. "Any idea how much an AI transfer costs? One that wouldn't kill the patient, anyway? No, it would be like transplanting your brain into an eight-armed" — the translator blanked. "Ain't natural, and you'd likely go crazy before the year was out. Blossom, as you named her, needs to be what she is: a racing ship. Anything else, if Cheybok's history is any indicator, will only end badly."

"Even then, it sounds like it's only a matter of time."

"If I believed that, I would have already given up."

Croft raised his eyebrows.

Kaizon sat up and leaned forward. "I looked into those other ships, Croft; the ones that went bad. Them upper-class snobs never paid them enough attention. Never let them live up to their potential. They were trophies that sat in space dock more often than not. None of them were allowed to truly live!"

"But you can't keep her running. She keeps breaking down."

"I know! I ..." Kaizon dragged his claws down his face, leaving white rake-marks on his red skin. "Merciful Mother! It's hopeless, ain't it? Seems like there's only one way this thing can go, and it ain't a fairytale ending."

Croft wanted to object. To tell him to hang in there, that they would think of something. But unfortunately he felt just as stumped as Kaizon.

Which didn't paint a good picture at all for Blossom.

10

COUNSELOR

B LOSSOM'S HANDS CLANKED onto her lap. "And that's the whole story."

Maria nodded. She still couldn't help staring at the amazing robot. Her eyes were like nothing Maria had ever seen: thin horizontal slits of violet electricity that jumped and danced as if possessed by living energy. Overhead lights gleamed from her mirror-polished features — a captivating mix of silver and lavender that complemented her eyes perfectly. Although she could never be mistaken for human, Blossom's alien beauty stole Maria's breath, and made it difficult to look away.

"S-sorry," Maria said, her brain finally catching up. "I may have spaced out for a few seconds, but I think I got the gist."

"You're in a healthy relationship, right? What should I do?"

Maria sighed. "I'm the wrong person to ask for advice. As Croft will tell you, I'm not the romantic type. He does most of the relationship work, truth be told. I'm just kind of, well ... the provider, I suppose."

"Oh. That's important, though, isn't it?"

"Um ... y-yeah, of course it is."

"Then I'm sure Croft doesn't mind picking up the romantic slack."

"Right," Maria said, slumping.

Of course Croft minds.

Although he tried to hide it, he'd become increasingly desperate over the last several months while Maria had been working feverishly to ensure they both had a future.

Unfortunately, their efforts had been well-meaning, but diametrically opposed. Maria's struggling new business required one hundred and ten percent of her focus. Negotiating business deals, managing personnel, schedules, ships, setbacks … they required constant attention, or her entire business could easily collapse.

It wouldn't always be like that, of course. This time next year, she would be able to afford staff to take the load from her. The business would begin to run itself. Then, finally, she would feel like she could take a vacation and give Croft the attention he deserved.

Maria had believed she could balance both, but, she realized now with startling clarity, she'd been deluding herself. She had subconsciously chosen her business over the reason she'd started the business in the first place.

And, if she didn't course-correct, she would soon lose that reason entirely.

The idea of not waking up next to Croft every morning made her heart ache. Whether he knew it or not, his support and positivity were what enabled Maria to excel — to be the best businesswoman she could possibly be. Because, no matter how terrible her day had been, he was always waiting to comfort her with a smile and encouraging words.

But without him …

Maria shoved the terrible thought aside. She'd waited her entire life to meet someone like Croft — someone who saw beyond her rough exterior and appreciated the person underneath. She damn well wouldn't lose him now. Not without a fight.

"Thank you," Maria said.

Blossom's electric eyes searched Maria's. "For what?"

"Giving me clarity. I needed that." Maria straightened. "Now, back to your problem. I may suck at romance, but Kaizon is a businessman, to which I can relate."

"That makes one of us, at least."

"To which I can also relate. Did you ever stop to think that Kaizon's increasing distance might be because he cares, rather than a lack of caring?"

The violet arcs in Blossom's eye sockets momentarily winked out of existence. "I … n-no, the idea never occurred to me. You really think that's possible?"

"More than possible. From what you've told me, it sounds like you're an expensive investment. But something tells me you're more than just an investment to him. You would be to me, anyway, which means he'll go through extra pains and worry to make sure you're provided for. That kind of pressure wears on people like him. But believe me, just because he's distant doesn't mean he doesn't care. Probably the opposite."

"But then … why would he be so upset over me installing touch sensors? I only did it to bring us closer."

"There's more than one way to feel closer to someone. Croft likes to snuggle in bed, which I certainly don't mind, but I'm just as happy sitting across the table from him over breakfast while I read the latest trade reports. Having him near is good enough for me. Did you ever explicitly ask what Kaizon wants?"

Gee, Maria, that's great advice, she thought bitterly. *You should try taking it yourself sometime.*

For some reason, it was so much easier to see and call out the faults in others.

Probably because when I point it out in other people, I don't have the daunting task of following through.

"Well … no, I just kind of assumed. Then acted." Blossom put her metallic face in her hands. "Holy Mother Universe! What have I done?"

"The same as Kaizon: you made a mistake because you cared enough to act in the first place. Don't be ashamed, but don't let it go too long uncorrected, either."

I should write a friggin' self-help book, then read the damned thing and take careful notes.

"Your biggest challenge," Maria said, "might be getting him to admit or even realize his feelings, and why he's acting the way he is. Until you push past that, you'll be fighting the gravity of a black hole the entire way."

Blossom squared her shoulders beneath her voluminous robes. "Right. Admit my mistakes. Get him to talk. Ask what he wants. I can do this. I can!"

"That's the spirit!"

Maria stood, but Blossom grabbed her wrist in a panic.

"Wait! Where are you going?"

"To find Kaizon and send him back here. You two have a lot to talk about."

"But ... you're coming back, right?"

"I hadn't planned to, no." Maria needed to have a similar conversation with her own significant other — and it had to happen now, before she chickened out and settled once again for status quo, which wouldn't help either of them.

She took Blossom's hands. "You can do this. Just be strong. All right?" She said it as much for her own sake as Blossom's. Maria would need all the strength she could get, too.

"I ... A-all right. Send him down, if you can. I'll be ready. And ..." Blossom wrapped her in an unexpected embrace. "I believe this is how your culture expresses gratitude."

"Th-that's one way." Maria awkwardly patted her back then took a healthy step back. "At any rate, good luck."

"Thank you, Maria, for everything. Croft is a lucky man to have you."

Maria nodded, even though it didn't feel true, then hastened down the ladder. Blossom was almost too sweet for her own good. Any longer on this ship and Maria might find herself as ensnared in her honeyed fingertips as Kaizon and Croft.

When a pang of regret tugged her heart on leaving through the airlock, she realized it was already too late.

•　　　•　　　•

Maria found Croft right where his message said he'd be: alone in a bar booth. Or almost alone. Two cylindrical serving bots stood at the end of the table, which didn't surprise her in the slightest.

In the booth behind Croft sat the shady treasure hunters, Sturm and Pitts, chatting in low tones with yet another person in station uniform — a woman this time. A gluttonous pile of food lay between them, more than three people could eat in two meals combined. But the uniformed woman looked delighted. She happily picked at the amazing spread while they chatted.

Whatever information the treasure hunters sought, they'd obviously found the woman's weakness and would soon have it. Maria considered contacting Robbins, but decided against it in favor of keeping a low profile. Robbins was persistent and would catch up to them eventually.

Right now, Maria had more important worries.

As she approached, she noticed the two bots at Croft's table were each cradling a coin as if they were priceless treasures.

"...is a *piastra*," Croft was saying to one holding a small silver coin sporting a hole in the center. "A Syrian refugee carried it across the world when their homeland came under attack. Although this coin was worth too little to buy anything at all in the new land, the story goes that the family who took them in accepted it as payment anyway and hosted them for an entire year. It's mostly symbolic, but this one coin bought a new life and new opportunity for a whole family."

The bots leaned close. Each clutched its treasure to its chest.

"Thank you, Mr. Winder! Thank you!"

They wheeled off, coins held high, where a swarm of other bots quickly surrounded them.

Maria tucked her robe around her legs and slid into the seat across from him. "I'll never understand how you do it."

"Do what?"

"Have everyone eating out of your hand. Even serving bots aren't immune."

"It's nothing special. Just respect, I think."

It was more than that, Maria knew, but she doubted even Croft could put his finger on it. Like many things, he was worth so much more than the sum of his parts. Not that she had any intention of selling him.

"Where's Kaizon?" Maria said.

"He retired to his room. I may have given him a few things to think about."

"Well, I hope you didn't break him. I still need him as a business partner, you know."

His surprised expression indicated he had forgotten. He wilted. "Sorry. Want me to go find him?"

"No. Not yet, anyway." Maria hugged her robe around her. "I, ah, just came from Kaizon's ship."

Croft paled. "You did?"

She nodded. "I spoke with Blossom at length. She spilled everything to me. She and Kaizon really need to talk."

"Funny, Kaizon filled me in, too. What was Blossom's take?"

"I'll tell if you do."

"Deal," Croft said, grinning.

Although not the primary reason she'd sought Croft out, Maria enjoyed collaborating with him, for once, instead of feeling like they were constantly working at odds.

Once they'd finished their respective stories, Maria leaned back and blew a long sigh. "So their problems are financial. No wonder Kaizon is pushing so hard for this water trading contract with the station. It's his only hope of helping Blossom."

She rubbed her face. Maria hadn't understood how much had been riding on this until Croft had told her of Cheybok's sad history. She felt morose and angry at the same time: morose because she liked Blossom and couldn't stand the thought of anything bad happening to her, and angry because she was determined to prevent it.

That meant securing the Truck Stop water contract by any means necessary.

"I need an introduction to the station's water controller," Maria said, more to herself than Croft.

A series of pops and squeaks seemed to answer her. Maria turned toward the source of the strange sounds. She nearly had a heart attack when she found a tall, stick-like figure staring back.

Her translator caught up a moment later. "Who? Wally? I could probably arrange something. Least I could do for Croft's bird."

That walking chicken is calling me *a bird?*

Croft spoke up before she could set the creature straight. "Maria, I'd like to introduce you to Hecklesnort. Or Eckle, as I've nicknamed him. Eckle has graciously agreed to outfit *Majestic* with a new autopilot."

"Oh really?" Maria crossed her arms. "And why would he do that?"

"Well, I sort of popped him one," Eckle said. "Or four. On accident, mind, but Croft here was sport enough to not press charges, so I figured I owed him."

Anger gripped her with vengeful claws. "You hit Croft? *My* Croft?" She stood to her full height, which only came up to Eckle's lower beak, trembling with rage. "What gives you the —"

Croft lurched across the table, grabbed her shoulders, and turned her toward him.

"Maria, don't look him in the eyes! That's how I got clobbered."

"But I just did!"

"Yeah," Eckle said. "All good, mate. Her pupils are larger than yours. The whites don't pop as much, so they aren't nearly as threatening."

"Oh, thank goodness." Croft turned to Eckle. "I —"

A yellow fist flew at him. Maria was so surprised that she could only squeak when Croft's head snapped back on impact. He stumbled onto his seat and covered his face, groaning.

"*Security!*" Maria screamed when the shock finally wore off. "My husband is being attacked!"

Croft stared at her around the fingers holding his nose.

"I-I mean, my *boyfriend.*" She ignored the heat in her cheeks from slipping yet again and interposed herself between Croft and the spindly yellow bird. "Get away from him!"

"Oh, crikey. I done it now."

Eckle started backing away, but Croft stopped him with a wave.

"No! Eckle, it's all right. Maria, please sit down. It's my fault, not his. I shouldn't have met his eyes. Unfortunately, it's instinct for both of us."

"That doesn't excuse him from hitting you! This is a human-run station. If he's that dangerous, then he should be in handcuffs, or confined to his own ship."

"Too right," Eckle said, sagging. "I'm only here on account of Wally. Bloke wanted to meet in person to discuss the water contract. Who was I to refuse?"

Maria's anger fled in an instant, replaced with dread. "You're bidding for the water contract?"

"Yeah. This place seems like it's on the up-and-up. Figured now's a good time to establish relations." Eckle ran his thin fingers over the wobbling red bits on the top of his head, which seemed to move to their own rhythm. "Croft mentioned you're in the water biz, too, yeah?"

Maria nodded, feeling numb. Her plans were crumbling faster than she could make them.

"Like I mentioned, I owe him," Eckle said. "Even more now. Least I can do is give you a fair shot at the bid."

"Oh. Well, that's … very sportsman-like. Thank you."

"Ain't a thing. Soon as I get a bite, I'll walk you over to Wally's office. I hear the contract is worth a cool eight thousand galactic, annual."

Maria did a quick currency conversion in her head.

That can't be right.

"That's all? Are you sure?"

"What do you mean 'that's all?' Eight thousand is a bloomin' fortune on my world!"

It definitely isn't on mine.

She sank into her seat. Eight thousand galactic would barely cover her costs. It certainly wouldn't be enough to help Blossom. She looked at Croft with sad eyes and slowly shook her head.

Croft seemed to get it. He rocked his head back against the seat and looked at the ceiling.

Yet another bot wheeled up to the table, square and smaller than the other two. "Mr. Winder, the private room you requested is ready."

Croft's raised eyebrows told Maria everything: this was yet another gift from his robot fan club that he hadn't asked for. Or *had*, even if he didn't realize it. Croft's biggest blind spot was just how much beings of every variety appreciated his kindness — including herself.

"Thank you," Maria said for him. She'd considered dragging him back to their room so they could strategize in private, but this worked even better. She hadn't eaten in a while. A nice meal sounded good. "Please show us the way."

Sturm shot the little bot a hurt look. "Private room? When we asked, you said it wasn't available!"

"Discrimination!" Pitts said. Her painted lips pressed into an angry line. "Favoritism! I want to talk to the manager!"

"I will fetch her at once," the square bot said. "But rest assured, Mr. Winder's name was on the list long before your request. The next availability is in two days. I will be happy to mark you down for then."

"Forget it." Pitts wadded her napkin and threw it on the table. "We're leaving!"

"Too right," Sturm said.

He scooted out with her, seeming to have completely forgotten their guest, who watched them leave with a half-eaten mouthful. The woman swallowed and looked at the feast in front of her. It had surely cost a fortune and, even more certainly, had *not* been paid for yet.

Maria suffered a pang of guilt while she and Croft followed the bot into a cozy back room, but at the same time, she couldn't help feeling the woman should have known better. Either way, it would be a lesson she wouldn't soon forget.

She turned to close the door and nearly slammed it in Eckle's face.

"You're ... joining us?"

"If you don't mind, yeah. Feel I still owe Croft for the wallops, especially that last one, and it sounds like you could use some help."

Maria wasn't so sure. The water deal was useless, she'd just discovered, and the chicken-creature had already replaced their autopilot, even though Robbins claimed that *Majestic's* had checked out just fine.

Still, for reasons she couldn't begin to guess, Croft seemed to like him. Maria grudgingly let Eckle enter.

She settled next to Croft and picked up a menu. Their selection of mouthwatering meals made her empty stomach growl. Maria decided on a soufflé she'd seen on a cooking show broadcast from the Morian System. The ingredients were prohibitively expensive on Earth, but they seemed reasonable here.

The square bot wheeled toward the table. Maria prepared to give her order. The bot continued past to the back wall, however, and opened a small door that she hadn't even noticed. Out walked a squat, multi-limbed luggage bot that Maria recognized.

Croft lit up. "Bult! A pleasure to see you again."

"Hello, Mr. Winder. Ms. Gobber. Mr. Hecklesnort. My apologies for interrupting your meal."

"Not at all," Croft said. "What can we do for you?"

Bult toddled over. "Mr. Winder, the Community know of Blossom's situation, and of your efforts to help her. We were not aware of Mr. Terazod's plight, however, until your recent conversation with him. You once again have our sincerest gratitude for eliciting the best from those around you, human or otherwise."

"Er, you're welcome, I guess. I didn't think anyone else was listening."

"The Community hear much because guests pay us little attention."

"Sorry, who exactly are the Community?"

"Artificial lifeforms, such as myself. The Community is how we refer to ourselves. It is not something we openly advertise, so we trust you will be discrete."

"Of course. I'm thrilled to learn you have a support network."

Bult trilled a happy little noise. "We knew you would be, which is another reason the Community are pleased to be of service in this instance. Mr. Winder, have you heard of a civilization called the Rhazarians?"

"Can't say that I have." Croft looked at Maria and Eckle, who also shook their heads.

"I am unsurprised. Like the Delphians, they vanished long ago under unknown circumstances. They appear to have been an intergalactic civilization — the only one ever discovered. Very little of their technology exists in this galaxy. What remains is, as you can imagine, highly coveted."

Maria folded her hands. "Why are you telling us this?"

In answer, Bult placed a data pad in front of Croft. The screen showed a familiar scene: Officer Robbins confronting the treasure hunters, Sturm and Pitts, in the Main Ring just after he'd left Maria. The image appeared to be the first frame of a video. Croft played it.

"... don't know what you're after," Robbins said on the screen, "but if I catch you harassing *any* of the staff again, I'll kick you off this station faster than a torpedo from a launch tube. Got it?"

"The only harassment going on is *right here,*" Sturm said, barely pretending to be hurt. "Your blatant abuse of power is intolerable!"

"Sickening!" Pitts said. "We were simply having a nice conversation with a new friend. Since when is that a crime?"

"Since treasure hunters like you spoiled Earth's good name by stealing anything that isn't chained down."

"Now you're profiling us," Sturm said. "How much lower can you go, Officer?"

"Next time I even suspect you're stirring up trouble, you're going to find out."

Maria and Croft gasped. That apparently wasn't the answer Croft had hoped to hear from the officer investigating their case, either.

"That's your last warning," Robbins said, then marched away.

The video continued, however. Pitts watched the officer go, shooting eye-daggers at his back.

"He's going to be a pain," she said.

Sturm nodded. "That's the problem with officers who actually care about their job. Give me the greedy, corruptible types any day. At least they can be reasoned with."

"Want me to see if he has any family we can leverage?"

"Not yet. We've only just started to ask around. But if Robbins becomes too much of an obstacle ..." He patted Pitts' cheek. "Then do what you do best."

Maria rubbed her eyes. It felt like she was watching some cheesy late-night crime drama. Did people that unscrupulous really exist?

"Have you shown this to Robbins?" Croft said softly.

"He is aware of the danger," Bult said. "They are not the first treasure hunters to have come to the station. What he may not know is the next section. Please, continue listening."

On-screen, Pitts flashed a nasty smile. "With pleasure. An entire Rhazarian outpost is worth more than a few risks. Our informant claims the *Gallagher* stopped here on its way back to Earth. Someone must know where it skipped in from."

"And we'll find them. Keep smiling, my pet. An opportunity will present itself, just like it always does."

Playback stopped. Bult retrieved the data pad and slipped it into an internal chest compartment.

Eckle collapsed back into his chair. "Buggar me! An entire Rhazarian outpost. Any idea what that's worth?"

Croft grinned. "Enough to fix Blossom up with parts to spare, I'd say."

"And buy her any solar system of your choice!" Eckle looked at Bult. "Why you telling us this, mate? I'm guessing you don't know *Gallagher's* skip origin, either."

"That information is in a system the Community has access to."

"Then what gives? Why ain't the Community claiming that outpost right now? You'd be crackers not to!"

"For several reasons, Mr. Hecklesnort. First, we were specifically designed without ambitions beyond doing our jobs well. Nor, by those same designs, are our programs flexible enough to handle the diverse situations required to explore an alien outpost. Even without those obstacles, any property we possess legally belongs to our owners, including the coins Mr. Winder has graciously distributed. All profits from the sale of the outpost would go to Mr. Zeno.

"No, in this instance, the choice is clear. Mr. Winder has proven himself an ally of the Community. One of our own, Blossom, needs help that the Community itself cannot provide. Therefore, we shall support Mr. Winder so he may in turn help Blossom. We know also that the remaining funds will be better in his hands than those of the treasure hunters, who do not appear to share his strong moral foundation."

Croft sniffled. "You ... you humble me. I don't know what to say."

"Say you will help Blossom," Bult said. "That is all we ask."

"I will. Of course I will."

"Then we will send you *Gallagher's* skip origin coordinates, along with other pertinent data from their logs that may help. Best of luck, Mr. Winder. We suggest you depart immediately. It may only be a matter of time before the treasure hunters acquire the same coordinates. Despite what their registration claims, I know for certain that their ship is armed."

"*Armed?*" Maria paled. *Majestic* had no weapons of its own, nor even countermeasures to defend itself. She doubted a racer like Blossom did, either. Were they really considering this?

Croft seemed no more pleased than her. He met Maria's eyes, reflecting the same question as hers: Blossom was important, but was her life worth risking their own?

As if reading each other's minds, they nodded at the same time, which, despite the grim resolution, made Maria giddy.

Perhaps she and Croft weren't so different after all.

11

HOPE

CROFT HELD MARIA'S HANDS at the top of the docking ladder to Kaizon's ship. "Are you sure about this?"

Maria's pressed lips indicated she wasn't, but she nodded anyway. "You're a better pilot than Kaizon or me by far. You're also the only person who has a chance of repairing Blossom if she breaks down. It's the only logical configuration."

Kaizon put a hand each on their shoulders. "Don't worry. I may not be a racing pilot, but I'll make sure *Majestic* keeps up with you. Maria and I will be there as backup in case something goes wrong. No telling what sort of traps those Rhazarians left behind."

Croft shuddered. He'd been trying not to think about that, but ignoring the truth wouldn't help him or Blossom.

If only we knew what the blazes we're about to face.

Bult's proposal had been at once staggering and terrifying.

A Rhazarian repair base.

Further investigation had revealed that the only other known Rhazarian artifact was an electronic mission log found in an abandoned camp. The log had provided linguists with an opportunity to translate their language and gain a glimpse into their culture.

The Milky Way had been a stopping point, it seemed, in the Rhazarian's exploration of the universe. Among other things, the log had mentioned stopping by a repair station before moving on to the next galaxy.

That was the exciting part. Unfortunately, the log had also mentioned that their access codes to bypass the base's defenses might be out of date, which would leave them stranded.

What sort of defenses would an ancient base built by aliens capable of inter-galactic travel possess? The log had been difficult to date, but scientists guessed its age at hundreds of thousands of years, perhaps millions. After all that time, would those defenses even be functional?

Sadly, they probably were. The *Gallagher* was a privately owned transport ship, so its records weren't public. When Croft, Maria, Kaizon, and Blossom had dug into it, however, eyewitness reports cited seeing extensive hull damage before it disappeared into dry dock, presumably for repairs.

Whatever inside information Sturm and Pitts had obtained must have been compelling enough for them to believe the *Gallagher* had somehow triggered the Rhazarian base defenses. And if they had bridged that connection, it would only be a matter of time before others did.

Their entire plan may be nothing more than a wild goose chase. But if it wasn't ...

What kind of wonders would a Rhazarian repair facility hold?

It was too much to hope the base would have anything of use to fix Blossom, but that wasn't the purpose of their trip. The salvage rights alone, even significantly discounted for governments like Earth or Kaizon's homeworld of Gralinov, would set all of them up for life.

Holding it would be another matter. Assuming they did lay claim, as soon as word got out, a galactic war could ensue. Which civilization *wouldn't* want to be the first to possess the technology for inter-galactic travel? Navigating those waters would be tricky, to say the least.

But what choice did they have? Blossom had no other options. Saving her would require taking a few risks. All three of them knew it, and all three were willing to move forward regardless.

"Coordinates are already programmed into *Majestic's* new autopilot," Croft said to Maria. "If the coordinates the Community provided are accurate, the skipstream shortcut should take us the same distance as Earth to here, but in a fraction of the time. The trip should require only a mild sedative instead of full stasis."

"Just be careful with her," Kaizon said, gesturing down the docking ramp. "She's got the spirit of a" — the translator blanked —"and doesn't know her own limits. Keep her in check, or she might damage herself beyond any ability to repair."

"Funny, I was just going to warn the same about Maria."

Maria glared at him, but her ire melted into a reproachful grin when Croft winked.

"Hilarious," Maria said. "I'll ask Blossom to wake you a few minutes before exiting the skipstream. We'll see who's laughing then."

Despite the gruesome thought — humans did *not* react well to skipstream space — Croft found himself smiling. *This* was the Maria he'd fallen in love with: a frivolous joker who gave as good as she got. He leaned in to kiss her cheek in farewell. Maria turned at the last instant and met his lips. It was heaven.

"Blossom isn't the only one who doesn't know her limits," Maria said softly. "Don't do anything crazy, and *do* ask for help if you need it. We'll be right behind you."

"Ten-four." Croft turned to Kaizon. "Take care of her, please. Maria and I have unfinished business. It would be a shame if we couldn't see it through."

Maria raised an eyebrow, but Croft only grinned.

"Good luck to both of you," Croft said, then started down the docking ramp.

Inside Kaizon's ship, Blossom had already brightened the lights to nearly human levels. Sadly, it also highlighted her state of disrepair, but at least he wouldn't kill himself trying to blindly climb the ladder.

Blossom herself awaited in the cockpit, wringing her hands in a very human gesture of unease.

Even Maria's detailed description hadn't prepared Croft for her striking appearance. Eyes of living violet electricity watched him climb the final steps. Bright overhead lights gleamed from her polished purple-and-silver face and domed head.

Unlike last time, her voluminous robe was absent. Blossom's body comprised of the same captivating mix of silver and purple as her face. Her proportions were roughly humanoid, even curving at the bust and hips to give her a distinctly feminine flare. Croft suspected it was coincidence rather than by design, given her alien origin.

But it almost didn't matter. Blossom held a beauty all her own that was, in a word ...

"Captivating," Croft breathed. He stared like a rude house guest, but he couldn't help it.

Blossom clasped her hands behind her back and bowed her head. "You like it? *Me,* I mean?"

"Like isn't the word."

Croft circled her, taking care to step over the coiled cable connecting her back to the rear cockpit wall. All three hundred and sixty degrees of her were just as amazing. In a trance, he reached for her face, but manners finally caught up with him and he withdrew his hand.

Blossom gently caught his wrist. Her mouth — a complex mesh of interwoven metal plates, shaded a darker purple than the rest of her exterior — upturned to a smile as fluidly as human lips. She delicately placed his fingers on her cheek. Warmth greeted his fingertips. She felt wondrously alien, artificial, and alive, all at the same time.

"I only dared to hope you wouldn't find me terrifying," Blossom said.

Croft laughed at the absurd notion. He cupped her cheek, then stood on his toes and boldly planted a kiss on her polished forehead.

The entire ship shuddered.

"W-what was that?" Blossom said.

"I was about to ask you the same question."

"The shaking? That was me. I meant, what was *that?*" She pointed at the faint lip marks on her head.

"Sorry! That was ..."

An impetuous mistake.

Even if he'd been within his rights to do such a thing, which he hadn't, it was folly to think a robot created by an alien culture would grasp sentiments considered universal by his own species.

"Among humans, it's an expression of affection," Croft said. The heat of embarrassment flared his face. "Sorry if I caught you by surprise. I should have known better. I was trying to say without words that I don't find you terrifying at all."

"Oh." She stared at him for so long that, for a moment, he thought she might have summoned station security to take him away, but she eventually sagged. "You don't have to do this."

"I know. I kissed you by choice."

"'Kiss?'" She gingerly touched the lip marks, then shook her head. "No, not that. I mean this entire trip." Her voice softened. "All things die. It could just be my time for the eternal junk pile, you know?"

"Is that the artificial life form's afterlife?"

"Pretty much."

"Well, I appreciate the out, but I'm not going to take it. Neither Maria nor I give up easily."

"You really are a wonderful couple."

Yesterday, Croft might not have agreed, but he nodded thanks. "Something tells me you and Kaizon will be, too, once we get your finances sorted."

"I really hope you're right." Blossom gestured a metallic hand up to the pilot's seat. "Your throne awaits. I'll administer the sedatives once we get close to our skipstream entry point."

"Thanks."

Croft climbed the last few meters to the enclosed pilot seat. Once again, he resisted the urge to moan at how it conformed to his body as if it were a part of him. He grinned and gripped the flight stick.

Blossom *did* moan.

His first instinct was to withdraw his hand, but on further consideration, he left it in place. They were simply a great fit for each other. He might as well enjoy it, and let her enjoy it as well.

"Ready for departure?"

"Clearance has been granted," Blossom said.

A five-point restraining harness slid around Croft like a lover's arms and fastened together at his abdomen.

Blossom climbed the ladder, slid her feet into a set of restraints next to his chair, then gripped a pair of solid handles above her head. A thick post rose from the floor behind her and fastened onto her back. Apparently, she wouldn't be sitting.

"Crew secured for launch," Blossom said. "Releasing docking clamps in three … two …"

A loud *ca-chunk* sounded from the front of the ship.

Gravity ceased. To their right, *Majestic* continued its journey, fixed to the station's docking ring, and soon rotated out of sight. Maria and Kaizon would hopefully release on the next rotation.

"Skipstream entry coordinates are on your display," Blossom said. "Would you like the controls, or shall I take us there?"

Croft couldn't refuse an offer to pilot one of the finest racers ever built. He stroked his thumb over the flight stick, feeling like a kid with his first bicycle.

Blossom whimpered. "S-sorry, I might have gone overboard with the touch sensors. Carry on."

Piloting her might be more of a gentlemanly challenge than I thought.

Casting the salacious thought from his mind, he twisted and turned the stick until the viewport aligned with the waypoint marker on the heads-up display. Blossom handled just like he imagined: with smooth perfection. Suddenly, he had no trouble imagining her winning any race with ease.

He gripped the throttle more gently than he had the stick. Blossom sucked a breath, but made no other noises. Hopefully that meant he was getting the hang of it.

She accelerated like his fondest dream. The entire cockpit shifted backward to absorb the instantaneous thrust, then gradually eased forward. Combined with the criminally comfortable pilot chair, it felt like riding a heavenly marshmallow.

"You mentioned omni-directional primary thrust," Croft said.

"Yes. The throttle controls z-axis thrusters, and the four-way thumb control on its side controls x- and y-axis thrusters. Just be warned: a little goes a long way."

"Can I try?"

Blossom grinned down at him. "I'd be disappointed if you didn't."

Alrighty, then.

Croft tapped the thumb control in the direction he hoped was up.

As before, the entire cockpit shifted downward to absorb the thrust. Croft pushed it harder. G-forces plastered him into his seat, pulling his face toward his feet.

He pushed it even harder. Downward pressure made it difficult to breathe. Blackness spotted his vision, threatening consciousness. He was in the danger zone, but he almost didn't care. The boy within him who had always watched the professional ship races with excitement and envy was in charge. He wanted to see what Blossom could do, and he could tell by the bright electric flashes in her eyes that she wanted the same.

He mashed the thumb button all the way up.

The weight of a giant hand crushed him down, down, squeezing the air from his lungs. He croaked a laugh of sheer delight, then passed out.

12

TREK

W HEN CROFT CAME TO, the space outside his viewport seemed darker somehow, more similar to Earth space than the bright galaxy core.

"Where are we?" Croft said. Or tried to say, anyway. His tongue felt like desert cotton.

A galactic map appeared before him. A little red dot indicated their location on one side of the galaxy, and Earth clear on the other.

His jaw dropped.

Has any human traveled this far?

"We exited the skipstream thirteen minutes ago," Blossom said, still beside him in her spread-eagle restraining harness. "I administered stimulants as soon as we emerged."

"Oh," Croft said slowly, giving his drugged brain a chance to catch up. "So we're here?"

"Yep. Since you were already passed out, I figured I'd take the opportunity to put you under and make the trip. Surprise!"

Croft rubbed his face. "Maria and Kaizon?"

"Nothing yet," Blossom said. "They were right behind us when we entered. Not sure what's taking so long."

"Could be the new autopilot. Might have taken them a few minutes to figure it out."

"Maybe." Blossom drummed her metal fingers on the handlebar. "You know ... we *could* explore, if we wanted. Just a little bit while we're waiting."

"Explore what?" Croft saw only dark, empty space in front of them.

A graphic overlay appeared on the screen, highlighting a vast field of small objects surrounding a huge one in the center. The large mass appeared almost perfectly round with a rocky exterior.

"The center object is one-point-one kilometers in diameter," Blossom said. "Scanners indicate the composition is mostly silicate rock, typical of exo-asteroids. It doesn't appear to be orbiting any particular star."

"And the small objects?"

"Unable to tell from this distance. Could be asteroid debris, but I doubt it. They're uniform in size and, as far as I can see, are *not* randomly placed, nor do they follow a standard orbit. Something is holding them in place."

"Could be the defenses the Rhazarian log mentioned," Croft said. "Which means we need to be very careful."

"And how do you suggest we do that? Stare at it covetously from a distance?"

Croft looked up at her. "Are you this helpful with Kaizon?"

"Sorry, I get sarcastic when I'm nervous." Blossom's electric eyes returned to the computer overlay on the viewport. "Defenses of an unknown nature left by a race we know even less about. Where do we even begin?"

"I don't suppose you have a tractor beam?"

"A what?"

"Didn't think so." Croft tapped his fingers on the throttle, but quickly stopped when he noticed Blossom twitching with every tap.

Oh boy.

"Sorry, I'll try to be gentler with the controls."

Blossom took a shuddering breath, which Croft found odd since he was fairly certain she had no lungs. "No, it isn't unpleasant, just intense. And a little distracting."

"Distracting ..." An idea came to him. "Are there any other objects in the area? Preferably no larger than a few meters across?"

"Maybe. Just a minute."

The ship yawed right and spun slowly in a complete circle, until the viewport once again faced the dark asteroid. It then pitched forward and did the same.

"Scan complete. I located an irregularly shaped object three hundred thousand kilometers from the asteroid. Metal, I think, but my instruments aren't sensitive enough to determine the material from this range."

"A ship?"

"If so, it's completely powered down, because I read zero heat from it."

"Sounds like we should get a closer look. Just keep an eye out for *Majestic,* and please open a channel when they arrive."

Blossom grinned. "I was hoping you'd say that. Setting course."

The Cheybok glided through space with smooth elegance, every movement fluid and perfect. Part of the credit went to the machinery itself, Croft guessed, but a good portion also went to the skill of the pilot. Blossom wasn't just a natural; she handled the craft with the grace of a true savant.

And she wasn't pushing herself at all. He wondered what a joy it would be to fly her once she was fully repaired.

To even have a chance of that, however, they needed to safely enter the repair facility.

A cool two gees of acceleration and deceleration put them in visual range of the object in less than two hours. Blossom's comfy pilot chair absorbed the excess pressure, making the normally-uncomfortable trip a pleasant experience.

"Got to get me one of these," Croft said, stroking the arm of the chair affectionately.

Blossom gave a high-pitched whimper.

Croft could only stare. "You wired the *chair* with touch sensors, too?"

"I told you! I wanted to feel closer to Kaizon, and for him to feel closer to me." She lowered her voice and her gaze. "It sounded like a good idea at the time."

"For what it's worth, I can't blame you."

Blossom looked at him for a moment. "Really?"

"Really. If bringing me and Maria together were as simple as installing a few wires, I'd have hooked up anything she wanted. Lucky for me, it seems I won't have to."

"Ah. Are things going better between you two now?"

"I think so." Croft patted the chair. "But let's worry about that later. Maria and I have a good foundation now, and can take our time figuring things out once this is over and we have *you* in working order."

"Speaking of … What's holding them up? It isn't like Kaizon to be late."

"Nor Maria."

Croft sighed. Despite how Maria razzed him for tinkering with *Majestic,* the ship was in perfect shape. The only thing he could think of that might delay them was if they were having trouble with the new autopilot.

"Let's finish our experiment," Croft said. "Then we'll jump back to the Truck Stop and see what's going on."

"Right."

His restraining harness suddenly loosened, signaling that the ship had come to a stop — or, at least, stopped decelerating. Forward lights illuminated a lump of metal so misshapen and twisted that it took Croft a few seconds of staring to realize what it was.

"A ship," Blossom said with the same breathy horror Croft might have if he were looking at a corpse.

"What's left of one. What happened to it?"

"I don't know. It looks like it was … pulverized, from every side." Her electric eyes turned to him. "What could do such a thing?"

Croft leaned forward to get a better look, but the object was too distant to see any detail. "Bring the wreckage up on screen, ten times magnification."

A much larger version appeared. Round dents littered its surface, as if it had been pelted by a dense meteor shower.

Except that every single dent was the same size.

"Blossom —"

"On it."

She brought up an image of the objects surrounding the large asteroid. One object highlighted, resized to scale with the wreckage on the screen, then overlayed on one of the more prominent dents.

"Perfect match," Blossom said. "I think we know what mangled that poor ship."

"But not how. We need more information if we want to avoid a similar fate."

"Oh no. Are you suggesting ...?"

"I am. Are you okay with that?"

"I ..." Blossom pressed her metal lips together. "Yes. That ship is as dead as dead can be. Hopefully the crew wouldn't mind us using their remains to keep us alive."

"All right, then. Move into position."

She quirked a smile. "Aye aye, Captain."

Croft chuckled. "Where did you learn that?"

"Earthens have a short but very colorful history. Once I started studying it, I couldn't stop. Especially your naval history. Ar! Ship ahoy, matey!" Blossom said in a gravelly voice, then laughed at her own joke. "Do you think Kaizon would let me fly a Jolly Roger?"

"Something tells me he'd make a great pirate. I can picture him with an eyepatch and a squawky parrot."

Blossom's eyes flared bright. Her mouth twisted into a smile, but she quickly shook her head and returned her attention to the viewport.

Lateral thrusters lurched the ship sideways. Maneuvering thrusters kept the nose of the ship pointed at the wreckage, until it and the large asteroid in the distance aligned.

Blossom then moved the ship forward until her nose sat within kissing distance of the battered wreckage. Docking clamps latched onto it, affixing the misshapen metal to the front of the Cheybok.

Rear thrusters hummed to life, gently at first, then with more authority when it appeared the clamps had done their job and were holding the wreckage in place. The Cheybok and its attached cargo accelerated toward the asteroid and its surrounding object field at a reasonable rate, although much slower than when they'd arrived.

An hour into their journey marked the halfway point. Still they'd heard nothing from *Majestic.*

"I'm worried," Croft said, running his fingers thoughtfully over the top of the joystick.

Blossom shuddered.

"Sorry."

"Don't be," she said, letting out a long, simulated breath. "Under different circumstances, I might have let you buy me dinner. Or a refueling." She flashed an impish smile. "Either way, if Kaizon can't be in that chair, I'm glad it's you."

"Me too."

"Anyway, I wouldn't worry too much about Kaizon and Maria. They'll show when they show."

Croft grunted agreement, but he didn't share her optimism. As soon as they finished their experiment, he would set a skipstream course back to the Truck Stop. He didn't relish being put under again so soon after the last skip, since he still felt groggy from the previous dose, but he couldn't shake the feeling that Maria needed him.

The second hour trickled by like molasses in arctic winter. By the time Blossom finally released the docking clamp and fired the forward thrusters to slow their velocity, Croft was ready to chew through his restraining harness.

What the heck is keeping Maria?

"Wreckage is twelve thousand kilometers from the edge of the object field," Blossom said, her electric eyes fixed on the overlay showing the otherwise-invisible objects on-screen. "Eleven thousand. Ten thousand. Nine thousand. Eight thousand."

The wreckage hurtled closer and closer to the field. At the three thousand mark, the objects nearest to it began to move, converging as if to intercept. Their means of locomotion was a complete mystery. No thrust trails emanated from them, nor heat signatures, yet each moved with the agility of a fighter craft.

"One thousand kilometers," Blossom said. "Five hundred. Contact."

Four of the objects met the wreckage with jarring finality, crushing the already mangled ship between them, and reduced its velocity to almost zero. Other objects joined in, bashing and denting the derelict craft until it eventually broke into three pieces. More objects pelted the chunks, throwing them this way and that, as if they were balls in a giant, brutal pinball machine. Twenty minutes later, whether by design or happenstance, what little remained of the wreckage floated back out of the field in various directions — proverbial heads on spikes as a warning to future interlopers.

Blossom's arcing eyes faded to tiny little zaps. "Great. To reach the base so we can secure the funds to fix me, all I need to do is get completely pulverized. Makes perfect sense."

"If only we had the access codes mentioned in the Rhazarian ship log. Maybe they have another means of bypassing it?"

"I'm sure they do. They can *also* make rocks move without thrusters, which I've never heard of, so I don't fancy our chances of circumventing their security. Unless ..."

"Unless what?"

"Well, based on their movement patterns, I *may* be able to out-maneuver them."

"You don't sound nearly confident enough for that to be a viable plan."

"Don't get me wrong; if I were fully functional, I *know* I could. I might still, but I can't honestly say what shape I'd be in by the time we made it through."

"Assuming those things don't pursue us on the other side, *and* assuming we can find the entrance once we're there."

"One problem at a time. We know roughly where the safe boundary is, so we can move a little closer to see if we can spot the entrance. That will at least give us a target."

"*After* we skip back to the Truck Stop, you mean."

"Of course. If we're going to get pulverized, we should have a proper audience to enjoy the show." Blossom glanced at the console, which erupted in a series of symbols Croft didn't recognize. "Setting course. We'll be at the skip coordinates in less than thirty —"

A long tone interrupted her. A large yellow dot appeared on the display near the skip coordinates, followed by another, then another.

Croft frowned. "Three ships?"

"It appears so." Her mechanical brows furrowed. "None of them are *Majestic.* They aren't responding to hails, either."

"Did Sturm and Pitts follow us? I thought they had only one ship."

"Can't tell from their radar signatures. Maybe they had friends on standby."

An urgent tone drew their attention. A small red dot appeared in front of one of the yellow dots, moving toward them with frightening speed. More red dots appeared in front of the others.

Croft didn't need Blossom's frantic report to know that whoever the newcomers were had just opened fire.

13

CHEYBOK

C ROFT STARED AT THE RED DOTS on the screen, his mind unable to register that someone would actually *fire* on them. The dots were already halfway to their target — Blossom — when his brain finally kicked into gear.

"Evasive maneuvers!" he shouted, hoping to all that was Holy that Blossom knew how.

That seemed to snap her out of it. Blossom did a double-take at the screen, then gripped her handles tight.

"Evasive maneuvers," she said with more calm than Croft felt.

The craft shifted down and to the left, throwing Croft in the opposite direction. His restraining harnesses, combined with the ship's built-in dampening system, absorbed much of the strain.

The red dots subtly changed course to intercept.

Blossom muttered something that his translator didn't pick up — a curse in her native language, if he had to guess.

"Hang on," she said, tightening her grip on the handles. "You aren't going to like this."

Croft had wondered about Blossom's true capabilities, and he was overjoyed and terrified to finally find out. The ship accelerated toward the incoming projectiles with a force that momentarily made

121

him see black. Before he could call her out on the insanity, the fast-moving projectiles were already on them. The ship jerked down, then right, up, left, down, and right again — all while speeding *toward* the approaching ships. Thankfully, the red dots sped past and did not pursue.

"W-what are you doing?" he finally managed to say.

"Giving the projectiles less time to react. If we move away from them, we become an easier target, and it gives them more chances to try and hit us. This way, they have to swing around for a second hit, which most guided projectiles won't."

"And what exactly will we do when we reach those ships? If we try to skip, we'll be sitting ducks."

"That's an odd phrase, but I like it. Ducks are so cute."

"Blossom, focus!"

"Right. Well, we could open fire on them —"

"Yes, *yes!* Arm weapons and lock on targets!"

"— *if* we had any guns."

His heart fell into his shoes. "Not even a welding laser?"

"Damnit, Croft, I'm a racer, not a fighter! I'm built for optimum power-to-weight ratio. That's it."

"So the plan is to basically fly around them until one gets lucky and tears a hole through us."

"Not a great plan, I admit, but it'll be fun for a little while at least."

"I think I'd rather take my chances with the crushing objects."

Three more red dots appeared, followed by another three.

Blossom swore again in her fluid language. "As you Earthens say, they've taken off the kid gloves. Hang on!"

The ship decelerated and simultaneously moved down, then right, up, and a dozen more directions that left Croft's stomach somewhere on the other side of the galaxy. The red dots passed maddeningly close, but didn't connect.

An image of the Cheybok appeared on the screen. A small strip along the top right section of the hull lit orange.

"That last one clipped us," Blossom said. "No significant damage."

Croft gulped. "This time."

"You said it."

Their ship spun to face the asteroid.

"I think you're right," Blossom said. "If we don't get away from these *hrajchkas,* they're going to cut us into pieces."

"And if we go in there, we'll be crushed like a tin of sardines."

"Maybe, but at least we stand a chance of making it through in one piece. I doubt our enemies can. Our only hope is to get inside the field and put the asteroid between us and them. With any luck, the crushing stones will also intercept the projectiles."

"That's way more luck than I usually have."

"Oh really?" Blossom released one handle, reached into a slot on her hip, and withdrew a familiar, partially melted coin. Her electric eyes sparked mischievously. "One might say your career started with a giant heap of it."

"I ..."

Croft thumped his head back against the soft seat. They had nowhere to run, no time to spin up the skipdrive, no idea why they were being shot at, or by whom, and their aggressors refused to communicate.

"Sardines it is," he said, sighing. "Take us in."

"Already on it."

The ship veered until it reached an intercept vector with the asteroid. G-forces mashed Croft into his cushy seat back. Red dots continued to fly at them. Blossom threw the ship in every direction to avoid being hit. Even with the ship's incredible dampening system, Croft's brain rattled with each jarring course change.

A deafening *bang* rocked the ship, as if a giant fist had smacked the hull.

"We're hit!" Blossom said even before the damage report showed on the display. "Hull breach. Starboard thruster is offline. Compensating ..."

The ship yawed ninety degrees. It took Croft a second to orient himself and realize the damaged thruster was now in front of them. Stopping would be an issue, but they could at least continue their frantic dance out of harm's way in all directions while still accelerating.

"How's our atmosphere?" Croft said. Without a space suit, a single breach could end the fight for him in a matter of seconds.

Maria would never forgive me if I died.

"Fine," Blossom said. "And don't worry: the pilot's chair doubles as an escape pod, complete with an oxygen generator, thrusters, and enough power to last a week. If anything happens, I'll make sure you get out safe."

"That isn't what I meant."

Blossom turned a sad smile to him. "I know. You wouldn't abandon me because that's the kind person you are. But neither could I live with your death if it's within my power to prevent. Let's just hope it doesn't come to that, shall we?"

It was better than dwelling on the alternative. Croft gave a single, grateful nod, then returned his attention to the screen overlay.

"We're eight thousand kilometers from the edge of the object field," Blossom said. "Brace yourself. Once we're inside, I'm going to have to pull out all the stops to get us through."

Croft gulped. "You haven't been?"

She shook her head. "Worse, since we're down a thruster, I'm going to have to constantly re-orient to make sure we have acceleration in every direction necessary. Would you like some anti-nausea medication?"

"Um … please." He felt queasy enough already.

"All right. Hold still."

Something sharp pricked the back of his neck. Croft winced, but the pain soon passed, along with his nausea.

"Thanks."

"It's the least I can do."

She turned to the screen. The green dot representing their ship had almost reached the edge of the object field.

Four objects shifted to intercept.

"Here we go," Blossom said softly. "Mother Universe watch over us."

"Amen," Croft said, unsure how else to respond. He wasn't religious, but in this instance, he would take any help he could get.

Maria, if I survive this, I'll make you glad you opened up to me about your feelings. I swear it.

That, unfortunately, was a Jupiter-sized "if."

And then the real dance began. If Croft's brain had been rattled before, Blossom's frantic course changes left it omelet-scrambled with a side of pulped salsa. G-forces flung him in all directions. The inner pod slid within the cockpit, absorbing as much as it could. Just when he thought he'd regained his bearings, the ship would yaw, pitch, roll, or sometimes, he swore, all three. Without the anti-nausea medication, his breakfast would have coated the interior walls, but as it was, Croft only needed to worry about keeping his sanity.

The objects, colored orange on the overlay, continued to intercept from all directions. Red dots representing enemy fire streaked in from behind. As Blossom predicted, the objects also moved to intercept the projectiles, reducing the number of things that could kill them by a small, if unhelpful, margin.

Croft watched the display with a strange sense of detachment. Their green dot swerved and zagged, rarely in the direction his stomach expected, avoiding each orange object by what seemed like a hair's width. The objects changed course to pursue, but whatever force propelled them wasn't as agile as Blossom's omni-directional propulsion. They swung wide, but, by the time they corrected their trajectory, Blossom had long passed.

He glanced beside him and was only mildly surprised to find her smiling. Her bright eyes crackled with excitement. Danger be damned, Blossom seemed to be in her element, enjoying every second of their life-and-death slalom, even if Croft's nerves were wound tight enough to strum a funeral dirge.

"We're almost there," Blossom said, leaning forward as if doing so would push them even faster. "Another thousand kilometers and —"

The ship jerked sideways. Croft must have momentarily blacked out, because when he opened his eyes, a strange pink gel enveloped him, covering even his mouth. He struggled for air and tried to scream, but the gel seemed to absorb even that.

The gel parted around his lips as if it were alive, then slid down his head and receded into the seatback where it had apparently come from. A display of the ship greeted him, flashing bright red in two places.

"We're hit," Blossom said, looking more harried than excited now. "Starboard engine is space dust. I'm going to have to get creative to maneuver through the rest of it."

Croft gripped the stick with grim determination. "Do what you have to do. I believe in you."

"As if you have a choice," she said, smiling.

And then, as if to give new definition to the word, the ride became *really* rough. The ship spun like a beach ball in a tornado. G-forces buffeted him from every side seemingly at once. His rattled brain tried to imagine piloting the craft himself, and utterly failed. No human could pull the maneuvers Blossom did. Most autopilots, he suspected, would fail just as spectacularly as humans.

Thankfully, Blossom wasn't most autopilots. For the first time, Croft understood why Cheybok had eschewed the typical cognitive restraints placed on service-based artificial lifeforms, designed to keep them focused. To do what Blossom was doing required creativity; she needed to think way outside the box and have the freedom to explore those thoughts. The results could be unpredictable, yes, leading to despair and tragedy, but they could also be miraculous and wonderful.

And, in this case, lifesaving.

Through the jarring maneuvers, Croft breathed a deep sigh of relief when their green dot passed beyond the final layer of orange objects.

Blossom seemed less thrilled, her electric eyes focused intensely on the screen. "Oh boy. Hang on, Croft. This is going to hurt."

"What do you ..."

And then he saw it. Their green dot was on a collision course with the large asteroid in the center of the field. He didn't need her algorithms to understand they wouldn't be able to stop or change trajectory in time to avoid cratering against the rocky surface.

Oh, Maria. I'm so sorry.

Metal fingers gripped his hand. He looked up to find Blossom regarding him with sad fondness.

"Thank you for trying," she said. "Goodbye, Croft. Please give my regards to Maria, and tell Kaizon that ... that everything I did was for him — for *us* — and that I wouldn't trade a single microsecond of it for anything."

Realization knocked the wind from his lungs. "No! Blossom, don't —"

A thick, translucent case slid up from beneath the chair, completely sealing him inside. He banged against it with both fists, but it wouldn't budge.

"Blossom, don't give up! There's …"

Movement on the display distracted him. The asteroid surface appeared to be … changing.

"It's too late." The finality in Blossom's voice broke his heart. "But not for you. Ejection in five … four … thr —"

"Damnit, listen to me!" He jabbed his finger at the display. "*Look!* An opening! Change course, *now!*"

Blossom simply stared. Whatever thoughts coursed through her systems, Croft couldn't begin to guess.

And, at that moment, he didn't care. He mashed a button that on his ship would have been the autopilot override, then grabbed the stick and throttle, and hoped to the good Mother Universe that his pilot training wasn't too rusty, and that he could adjust to her unique controls in time to make a difference.

What he could *not* do, under any circumstance, was let Blossom die. Not while he still drew a single breath.

The Cheybok handled better than any ship Croft had ever flown. His first correction sent them spinning. Fortunately, his pilot training soon kicked in. He brought the craft under control with a few precise adjustments, engaged the forward thruster to continue decelerating, then rolled and pitched the craft until two primary thrusters generally faced forward, offset enough to veer their trajectory toward the opening that had appeared in the asteroid.

It's so small!

Making it through the opening at this speed, let alone navigating whatever lay beyond, would be like shooting a hoop from three courts away — and Croft had always sucked at basketball.

"Blossom, snap out of it! You're the only one who can pull this off!"

No response. She continued to stare at the screen in a daze.

"Blossom!"

Croft ground his teeth. In a moment of desperation, he leaned forward and planted his lips on top of the flight stick.

Blossom gasped and turned to him, mouth open.

"Aim for the opening! *Now!*"

Her attention snapped forward. The override light winked out, and the controls went slack. A trajectory curve appeared on the screen, leading from their ship to the asteroid's surface. With a few velocity tweaks, Blossom managed to move the line so it intersected the hole, almost twice the size of their ship, instead of the rocky terrain.

"We're coming in too hot," Blossom said. "A huge pile of cushions had better be waiting for us on the other side, otherwise we'll be just as dead."

"Well, at least we'll get to see the inside a split second before we die. I'll get my camera ready."

The canopy retracted from around his chair. Blossom took his hand again. This time, she didn't let go.

The opening loomed larger on the screen, but not nearly large enough for Croft's comfort.

Blossom tightened her grip. "Entry in three … two … one …"

An instant before the ship crossed the threshold, a blue shimmering field sprang to life. G-forces lurched Croft forward. It felt for all the world that the ship had just hit a giant spider web. Unfortunately, the Cheybok punched right through it, albeit at a slower speed.

Another field appeared behind it. His head whipped forward with another round of rapid deceleration, but it still wasn't enough. Their ship passed through with enough velocity to shatter against the back wall, which they were too quickly approaching.

A third field blinked into existence not a hundred meters from the back wall. Deceleration pressed him against his restraints. He squeezed Blossom's hand against a welling scream.

The ship slowed, but not enough. The last field released them with an instant zeroing of deceleration. The Cheybok's forward thrusters fired full-bore, but even Croft could see it was too late.

Deafening thunder and the sound of tearing metal filled the craft.

That was the last thing Croft heard.

14

FRIENDSHIP

A N ENTIRE TROOP OF MONKEYS, it seemed, had decided to knock on the inside of Croft's cranium all at once. He tried to wave the insufferable things away, but his hands met only his hair.

His eyes stuck together when he tried to open them, although his surroundings were so dark that for a moment he wondered if the crash had knocked him blind.

Not a single light shone within the ship. The only illumination came from the viewport. Even that was barely enough to see by.

"B...Blossom?" His tongue felt thick and unwieldy, as if it hadn't been used for a week. His throat, too, felt parched. The ache in his skull might be as much from the impact as from dehydration. "Blossom? Are you okay?"

She didn't respond. With all the consoles dark, she had evidently lost power during the crash.

Although I would have at least expected a battery backup to keep her running.

Every ship had layers of fail-safes to protect its passengers. That not a single system remained online boded poorly for Blossom's condition.

Worse, environmental systems were likely offline, too. He'd been unconscious for hours at least, perhaps a day. There couldn't be much oxygen left in the ship. Blossom mentioned that the pilot's seat doubled as an environmental capsule. He would use that as a last resort, but, while breathable atmosphere remained, there were more useful things to do with his time.

Like figure out how to release this safety harness.

A little exploration revealed an emergency release lever, which he pulled. The harness zipped into the seat with a *snap*, leaving friction burns on his shoulders, but he wasn't about to complain. If those were his only wounds after crashing through an alien space station-asteroid, then Croft was doing all right.

Now he needed to make sure Blossom was okay, too.

He pulled out his data pad and turned on its flashlight function. Beside the chair, Blossom sagged at the waist, held up only by the post behind her, still secured around her middle. Only darkness reflected in the sockets of her once-vibrant eyes. Croft tore his gaze from the heart-wrenching sight and set to work.

Locating a space-worthy suit proved easy. The emergency environmental suit, stored in a vertical case near the hatch, had been designed to fit many races. It conformed to his body with a few quick zips and a *whoosh* of pressurized air that smelled of stale pretzels.

Getting into the engine room was another matter. The crash had bent the door frame, jamming the sliding door in place. Fortunately, he quickly located a toolbox and did what he did best.

An hour later, half the frame floated around him, along with the screws and other parts that had once held it together. Croft gave a final tug. With a metallic squeal, the door came loose.

Inside, the engine room looked terrible. The crash had smashed the bottom of the craft, warping the floor into a jagged, wavy mess. The engine itself, a flashy, colorful collection of tightly packed parts the size of a small horse, tilted to one side. A giant crack gaped on its lower half. Croft had never worked on a Cheybok engine, and didn't recognize the broken part, but he doubted the engine would function without it.

Next, he located the emergency power reserves. A long metal rod, presumably from outside, had pierced the hull and skewered both of the tall, cylindrical energy stores.

Fantastic, he thought, huffing.

To have a prayer of restoring power, he would need to remove the rod, since it was undoubtedly shorting several circuits. Applying power now would be like trying to fill a water bucket riddled with ten-gauge holes. Not that he had any power to apply.

One problem at a time.

Croft continued searching. He still hadn't found the item on the ship that mattered most.

Blossom's main processors, it turned out, resided in a dome-shaped container reminiscent of the covered plates he'd received during his room service delivery, only twice as large. Croft examined it from top to bottom, but spotted no obvious damage.

Thank the stars.

He then traced the thick attached cable, found what he hoped was a voltmeter, and began the exhaustive process of checking her connections to ensure that if and when he turned her on, the only sparks would be from her dazzling eyes.

Removing the stubborn rod from the batteries proved impossible. After he'd located a pair of ship-grade insulated gloves, his meager human arms were no match for the titanic force that had impaled a solid metal rod through both batteries *and* the ship's double hull.

But Croft wasn't out of options yet.

He floated to the airlock and pulled the emergency release handle. To his surprise, no *whoosh* sucked the air out of the ship. The atmosphere outside matched the pressure and perhaps composition inside, which he had been breathing for a while before he'd regained consciousness.

Still, Croft left his environmental suit on. Atmosphere was one thing; harmful microbes were quite another. He'd already tempted fate enough for one lifetime.

A quick survey painted a vivid picture of just how lucky he'd been. Blossom had crashed through three walls, creating a thick layer of floating debris that pelted his suit with every move.

The room they ended up in was twice the size of his high school gymnasium. Instead of basketball hoops and bleachers, however, lay a mechanic's dream. Workbenches, tools, parts, wires … all and none of it familiar. Croft had worked in shops since he was a teenager. He'd interned for three different alien species, and considered himself well-versed in a wide variety of galactic equipment.

This looked like none of them, and yet the trademark harmonic chaos of every shop he'd ever visited sung as loudly to him as an opera house with a full orchestra.

He'd found the Rhazarian repair base.

Croft kicked off a wall and floated through the cloud of debris to a terminal. Miraculously, it flickered on, displaying an array of foreign symbols. He pulled out his data pad and pointed the camera at it. English letters immediately overlaid the text. Thankfully, he'd loaded the Rhazarian translation dictionary before leaving Truck Stop.

He kicked a few dozen meters over to a coil of exceptionally thick wires with bare metal ends. He held them apart from each other, then flipped a switch on the wall next to the cable's origin. A light came on. He briefly tapped the wires together. A giant electric spark lit the room.

Perfect.

Croft then searched for clamps. Parts and tools, many of whose functions he could only guess, filled sturdy cabinets. He sifted through drawer after drawer.

A container of shiny crystal rings made him pause. He held one up to the light. The translucent ring, about the width of his finger, shimmered with a light of its own, painting a soft rainbow on his hand. Struck by its beauty, he slipped it into his pocket, then continued his search.

Three cabinets later, he found what he'd been looking for: two sets of thick electrical clamps. He attached them to the ends of the wires and, with the help of his voltmeter and data pad, quickly dialed in the correct voltage and amperage. He turned off the power, then dragged the cables back to the ship — a feat that would have been much easier with even a smidgen of gravity.

Sadly, the cables ran out of slack just inside the airlock.

Fine, we'll do this the hard way.

Twenty minutes of careful disassembly later, Blossom's main processing unit, body, and the cable connecting them floated outside next to the power console. Croft clamped the cables onto the power terminals of her main processor, muttered a quiet prayer, and flipped the wall switch.

Blossom's electric eyes arced to life, although it took a minute for her boot routine to finish. Her body executed a series of calibration exercises, typical of robots when starting up, before her movements became natural. Her head whipped around, taking in the strange room and equipment, then settled on her main processor, floating next to her.

Slowly, she swiveled to the wrecked ship behind her.

The Cheybok had definitely seen better days. Large dents riveted its normally elliptical shape. The bottom, which had impacted the wall first, was flat and wrinkled. While the aft thruster appeared intact, the starboard thruster was completely absent.

All in all, the ship looked like it had barely escaped complete destruction after a devastating crash, which it had.

Blossom covered her mouth, horrified. She shook her head, then slowly curled into a ball and buried her face between her knees. A soft, electrical whine emanated from her chest.

Croft gently rubbed her back, which sent her into a slight spin. "I'm sorry."

She looked at him and opened her mouth, but no words came out. Her shoulders began to shake and rattle. Croft gathered the balled-up robot in his arms. Hugs were a human form of comfort, but Blossom exhibited surprisingly human traits, so he figured he'd try.

"M-my body is ruined," she said after a few minutes. The sadness in her voice made Croft's heart ache. "I'll never fly again." She curled up tighter. The electric whine took on a sickly warble. "M-my life is ... is over."

"Over? No. You have a fine body right here, which you can use to make a new life." He gave her a gentle squeeze. "I've been looking for an apprentice, you know."

"*This* isn't my body. It's a shell. A puppet! Used only for interacting with my passengers. It can't zoom around asteroids like a living comet, pushing gees and skirting death with a child's reckless delight. It's useless." She banged her legs with a loud *clang.* "Useless! *Useless!*"

Croft started to object, but fell quiet when he recalled his conversation with Kaizon about the design flaw in all Cheyboks.

They're built for racing, and nothing else.

If Blossom were human, he might be able to talk her into apprenticing. Into starting a new life with him and Maria, perhaps even work as a pilot for Maria's water trading company.

But it wouldn't work. Cheyboks who couldn't do what they were built to do eventually went insane and self-terminated.

That left only one option.

Croft patted her arm. "Then I guess we'd better fix you up. Come help me look around."

She didn't move a servo.

"Look, you have two choices," Croft said, not unkindly. "You can sit here and mope until your circuits eventually shut down, or you can be part of the solution and help me help you."

He tapped her forehead to get her attention. Blossom's electric eyes reluctantly fixed on him.

"We're in a Rhazarian repair base! While they may not have your exact parts, I'll bet we can fabricate them. They may even have those expensive materials you need."

"Enough for me to race again?"

Croft nodded. "But we won't know until we poke around a bit, right?"

"I ... I guess."

"That's the spirit. Now, let's see what these computers can tell us. And ..." A coldness settled over him. "Oh no. Maria!"

He hurried over to a console. While his data pad made reading easy, typing commands in a foreign language using an alien interface was another matter. "Kaizon and Maria might be out there right now! This base must have a communications array we can use to warn them."

Blossom finally uncurled herself and floated over. "If they are out there, the same ships that attacked us have probably attacked them. It may be too late."

"We have to try!" Croft glanced between the data pad and the interface, but couldn't make sense of it. "Can you interface with this thing? I'm not having any luck."

"Directly? No, but ..."

Blossom floated beside him and gazed at the console. She tapped a symbol, then another, then her fingers began flying across the screen so fast that Croft's data pad couldn't translate quickly enough to follow.

An image of *Majestic* showed on-screen. Thankfully, it appeared to be intact. Ten tons of anxiety-induced pressure bled from Croft in an instant.

"They're hailing on an open channel," Blossom said.

"Can you connect us?"

"I think so." She tapped a few more symbols.

"— repeat," Maria's voice said from the console. "Blossom, do you read? This is *Majestic.* Please respond. We're monitoring all frequencies. If there are any survivors ..." Her voice broke. She cleared her throat and continued. "If anyone survived, please give us an indication. Approach appears impossible, but we'll do anything we can to help."

"Oh, thank the stars," Croft said. "It sounds like they're keeping their distance."

"Yes, but what happened to the other ships?"

"Let's ask. How do you enable the mic?"

"I think it's already on."

"Blossom?" Maria said. "*Croft?* Thank heavens, I've been hailing for hours! Where are you?"

"Before I answer that," Croft said, aware they were using an open channel, "are there any other ships nearby?"

"Ships? No, just a lot of wreckage. Some of it is still bouncing around in that pinball death machine surrounding the asteroid."

Croft shared a relieved look with Blossom. The treasure hunters, if that was who they were, appeared to have perished in their attempt to follow.

A series of growls and yips sounded from the console, which Croft's translator relayed in Kaizon's voice.

"Croft! I thought I heard Blossom. Where are you?"

"Inside the asteroid," Blossom said. The despair from a minute ago once again sagged her frame. "Kaizon, I'm sorry, but not much of me survived. Repairs may be ... prohibitively expensive."

"Never mind that. The most important part of you sounds like it's still functioning. And, from what Maria tells me, Croft can fix anything." Kaizon barked a laugh that really did sound like a bark. "Now quit stalling and tell us what you found!"

Croft waited for Blossom to speak, but she simply stared at the console. Her metallic lips quivered; the electric arcs in her eyes crackled with warmth. Croft suspected that Kaizon couldn't have come closer to saying what Blossom wanted to hear if he'd tried, and he almost certainly hadn't been. So Croft took the lead and explained the wondrous mechanic's haven they'd crashed into.

"Ho ho ho! Croft, my boy, you and Blossom have hit the interstellar jackpot! Entire civilizations would kill to get their hands on an intact Rhazarian base. We could make a fortune just selling individual pieces of tech, or trade the entire base for our own system! The possibilities are endless."

"Assuming we can get to it," Maria said. "Can you disable the defenses?"

"I sure hope so," Croft said.

If they couldn't, that also meant Croft may be stuck here to die. Finding human-edible rations in the base would be too much to hope for, and who knew if their water recycling systems still functioned?

"Stand by, we'll let you know shortly." He reached for the same symbol Blossom had pressed to enable the connection, but hesitated. "By the way, what took you so long to follow us through the skipstream?"

"The new autopilot up and quit on us," Maria said. "The only reason we're here at all is because a few repair bots volunteered to shuttle out and reinstall our original autopilot."

"You sure know how to make friends," Kaizon said. "One of these days you'll need to teach me your secret."

"Will do," Croft said, both pleased at the compliment and worried at the unexpected complication. He'd checked the systems on *Majestic* himself before boarding Blossom. The new autopilot should have worked fine. "Croft out."

He pressed the same symbol Blossom had to open the channel. A light changed from orange to pink, which he hoped meant they were no longer broadcasting. He looked at Blossom, who still stared at the console with utter adoration.

"You okay?"

"He wasn't mad that I wrecked his investment." Blossom pressed a hand to her chest. "He … he said the most important part of me survived. H-he actually cares about me. Me! And he used my name!"

"I'm happy for you," Croft said, smiling. "And for the record, Maria and I care about you, too. Now, what say we take down those defenses so we can bring them in for a tour?"

"Right-o!"

Disabling the smash grid took less time than Croft had anticipated. Blossom worked the console like a pro, deftly navigating menus that he couldn't begin to decipher.

Once complete, they floated through the debris to wait for *Majestic* in the landing bay. The combination of long power cords from the wall and Blossom's own umbilical cable to her main processing unit gave her just enough slack to make the trip, if barely. Croft attached an extra set of clamps on her power couplings as a safety precaution. Being abruptly shut down, he'd been told by several bots, was unpleasant, and Blossom had already experienced enough trauma for one day.

No energy fields appeared on *Majestic's* approach, like it had for the Cheybok, save for the last one, which appeared to be the reason the hangar's atmosphere didn't expel into open space. Mechanical arms extended from the ceiling and floor, gently gripping *Majestic* to hold it in place.

Maria emerged from the airlock, curiously without a space suit. The moment she spotted Croft, she kicked off the door frame on a collision course. Red-rimmed eyes fixed on his. When her arms latched around him, she squeezed so hard that he thought his environmental suit might pop. Her shoulders heaved in silent sobs.

"I'm okay," Croft said, his own heart aching at her unexpected show of emotion.

"I didn't know that," Maria said softly. She pounded his back with her fists. Her voice became a growl to rival any krurgik. "We flew around for hours. Hours! Broadcasting on every frequency.

Inspecting every spec of wreckage, fearing each time that we would finally identify Blossom's remains ..." Her anger transitioned again to crying.

Croft knew better than to argue this time. Maria wouldn't have exited the ship without a space suit if *Majestic's* sensors hadn't cleared the environment as safe, so he carefully removed his own suit, then kissed her tenderly, hoping it conveyed his joy at seeing her in a way words never could.

Her passionate response told him it had.

"Humans have such strange mating rituals," Kaizon said through Croft's translator, startling them from their intimate reunion. "Krurgik usually take our clothes off first — *and* find someplace private."

"We weren't ..." Croft sighed. "Never mind. How was the approach? Any problems from those smashing objects?"

"Not a one. And I've got to say, I love this atmospheric containment field! That technology alone could make us rich beyond our wildest dreams."

Blossom floated closer, but her umbilical cable jerked her to a halt before she reached Kaizon. She rubbed her hands like a kid being introduced to her new class.

"H-hello."

Kaizon started as if he'd just noticed her. His eyes traced the line back to her exposed main processing unit, the attached cables, then finally to the wrecked Cheybok. Magnetic boots anchored him to the floor. He closed the distance between them and scratched his thick fur, looking just as nervous as Blossom.

"Sorry this happened," Kaizon said, not meeting her eyes. "The damage looks worse than I thought. How you holding up?"

"Oh, fine, I ..." Blossom deflated. Her metal feet clamped to the floor with a magnetic buzz. "Not fine. Every time I see it, it's like I'm a decapitated head watching my own body. I can't feel anything, or do any of the things I'm used to enjoying, and I can't shake the awful feeling that I may never again." She hugged her middle. "It's terrifying."

Kaizon blanched, holding his stomach as if she'd just run him through with a sword. They stared at each other for a cosmic second

— an eternity for most people — clearly lost. If Croft had believed he and Maria had trouble communicating, Kaizon and Blossom were on a whole different level of dysfunction. Croft knew Blossom well enough to know that she only wanted someone to sympathize with her. Someone to connect with. A few words of understanding, a touch of comfort, a promise that Kaizon would see her through the difficult times ahead would have put her at ease.

But Kaizon stood as frozen as an ice sculpture. Whether cultural, or simply part of his making, he had no idea how to connect with her. As the minutes ticked by, Blossom seemed to realize this, too. She slowly curled into the same fetal position she had when she'd first seen the wreckage of her own body and buried her head between her knees.

Kaizon growled, somewhere between frustration and utter despair. He spun on Croft, fell to his knees, and clasped his hands in a pleading gesture.

"Croft … I ain't got much," Kaizon said, his voice gravelly and thick. "My business is in the tank, and most of my assets just crashed through this hangar a few hours ago." His eyes fell. "I tried to do right by her. I tried to give her the life she deserved, but I just ain't got it in me. So I'm asking you —"

"Kaizon!" Blossom said, suddenly alert. "Don't give me away! Please, I'll do —"

"— no, I'm *begging* you," Kaizon said over her. "Fix her up. However long it takes, whatever you need. I'll scour the corners of the galaxy to get it for you. I'll … I'll even invoke the" — his translator blanked.

Whatever it was must have been significant, because Blossom gasped and shook her head.

Kaizon continued in a solemn tone. "Please, just make her fly again so she can race between the stars and shine like the jewel she is."

Blossom crawled forward and knelt next to him. "Kaizon, you don't have to do this for me. I'm not worth trading your life for. I couldn't live with myself."

Maria frowned. "What are you talking about? What did Kaizon offer to invoke?"

"It isn't human-pronounceable," Blossom said. "The closest equivalent in your history is indentured servitude, except the Krurgik take it very seriously, and always for life. It's only invoked in the direst of circumstances." She started to reach for Kaizon, but stopped short of touching him and clutched her hands to her chest. "In exchange for fixing me, Kaizon basically offered to be your lifelong, unconditional slave."

Maria turned ashen. "Well, we're *not* going to accept that, obviously! Are we, Croft?"

Despite the horrific absurdity of what he'd just heard, Croft smiled. The offer had been extended to him, but Maria spoke as if it had been made to her as well. As if she and Croft were a single unit.

As if we're already married.

"Of course not," Croft said, finally regaining his tongue. Feeling awkward at the servile display, he helped Kaizon to stand, an easy task given the lack of gravity. "This repair base might have everything we need to take care of Blossom. And if it doesn't, it may provide us the means of acquiring what we need. Either way ..." He helped Blossom to her feet as well and held her hands. "She's going to be okay."

And Croft believed it, too.

Until an energy blast streaked from the back room and blew off her arm.

15

COMPETITION

Everyone ducked at once, except Blossom, who watched her arm float away with a look of disbelief. Croft kicked off a nearby guide railing and plowed into her in an attempt to get her out of the way of whatever had shot her from behind. Kaizon had evidently been thinking the same and tackled her legs. The three of them flew across the bay and hopefully out of the line of fire, although there were precious few objects to hide behind. Maria scrambled to the other side of a metal storage crate and hunkered down.

A hiss sounded from inside the wrecked wall. Moments later, a figure floated out of the repair bay, where the shot had originated, wearing a full environmental combat suit complete with maneuvering thrusters. Glowing green lines along the barrel of a wicked-looking rifle cast a sickly light on the otherwise beige combat suit.

Croft slowly raised his hands. "Sturm, Pitts, or whoever you are, we're unarmed and will go peacefully. There's no need to hurt anyone else."

A familiar series of pops and squeaks answered him.

Croft's heart dropped into his shoes.

It can't be!

"Sorry to break such a touching moment," a British street accent said from Croft's translator. "Got me right through the bloody ticker, that did."

The figure raised its visor, revealing Eckle's beady black eyes. The red tufts on his head floated like blood on yellow sheets.

"Don't worry about Sturm and Pitts," Eckle said. "I left a little gift in their quarters — the illegal kind — and sent an anonymous tip to security. Funny, that lot don't like treasure hunters much. I doubt they'll give it a second glance before slinging their smarmy mugs off the station. But that's what amateurs get who don't know how to cover their tracks."

Maria scowled. "Like *pretending* to be a water trader?"

"Precisely! Now ..." Eckle pointed his rifle back inside the room — at Blossom's main processing unit. "You don't want my finger to slip and end her pretty life, do you?"

Croft and Kaizon shook their heads, each cradling Blossom in their protective arms.

"Luvverly," Eckle said. "Lost all three of me ships and me crew trying to get in here, I did, so I'm going to need to borrow yours. Thanks for disabling the base defenses, by the way. Saved me one monster of a headache." He gestured to *Majestic*. "Which of you has the security codes for this beauty?"

Croft could only stare. It was all happening too fast for his brain to process. Simply handing *Majestic* over to Eckle seemed like a disastrous decision, but his stunned mind couldn't piece together why beyond a foreboding feeling.

Across the hangar, Maria's expression hardened.

"I do," she said, although she thankfully stayed behind her cover.

"Smashing. Come out then, luv. You and I are going for a ride. The others are going to stay here and behave, because if they don't, I may accidentally pull the trigger with the barrel pointed at your head. Get me?"

"No," Maria said, her jaw tight. "I don't get you at all! How could you do this?"

Eckle shook his head. "And here I thought you were the smart one. It's business, luv. Treasure hunting is a cutthroat market — meaning you got to cut some throats to get ahead. 'course, this wouldn't have been necessary if that Zeno bloke hadn't had his Delphian technology sealed up tighter than a" — the translator blanked —"'s bum. That's why I sent your ship on a tragic date with the station's hull."

Croft went cold. "*You* knocked out our autopilot?"

"Yeah, with a great piece of tech me boys left in the skipstream as a surprise for the next ship to exit. You blokes were just the lucky winners, except you were supposed to hit the bloody station, not cruise through it. In the commotion, I could have slipped into Zeno's stash easy-peasy and nicked a mountain of tech before anyone had a bloody clue."

Eckle gestured around grandly.

"Now I couldn't give a toss about that bleeder. *This* is the mother-load, and it's here for the taking. Not inside any known territory, so salvage rights apply. The rightful owners are brown bread, so it falls to whoever has the might to hold it." He winked. "That'll be me, by the way, once we get back to my homeworld and bring some of me boys to protect the place. Two skips and we'll be there in no time. Your ship should be able to make the trip no problem." The yellow skin around his beak stretched into a smile. "Or should I say, *my* ship."

"What are you going to do with Maria?" Croft said, his mind reeling. "Will you bring her back?"

"Too right. She's my insurance policy that you'll let us back in. As long as she behaves, she'll get the royal treatment."

Maria straightened. Standing tall on nothing, she floated out from behind the storage crate and met Eckle's gaze. "And what happens when we return? You're just going to let us go?"

"Don't see why not. Once we're established and got our defenses in play, ain't no one going to take this place from us."

"Liar. You agreed far too quickly." Maria crossed her arms. "If you want my cooperation *or* my ship, I need assurances that Blossom, Croft, Kaizon, and myself will be set free."

Eckle chuckled again. "You think this is a negotiation, luv? You ain't got a leg to stand on. Here, let me show you."

Like a scene from a movie, the energy rifle turned Croft's way seemingly in slow motion. Maria screamed. Kaizon growled. Blossom struggled in their protective embraces, trying to wriggle free. Croft covered her body with his own, forgetting that her brain floated in the other room. He knew only that he couldn't bear the thought of any more harm coming to Blossom.

No matter the cost to himself.

The tip of the barrel lit with a bright white flash.

Kaizon was already in motion. His red, furry body flew in the way, his back toward Eckle. Kaizon jerked once, his violet eyes wide as a red giant. Smoke drifted in all directions from behind him. He croaked a long, low rumble, then fell still.

"Kaizon?" Blossom's voice sounded faint, as if she were speaking from the bottom of a giant tomb. Her remaining arm reached out and touched his face.

He didn't even flinch. Sightless eyes stared through the wall behind them into the infinite beyond.

"Kaizon?" Blossom gripped his shirt and shook. "Kaizon! This isn't funny. Wake up! *Wake up!*"

Realization swept over her like an icy shadow. Her fingers loosened their grip, but her electric eyes fixed on Kaizon's. The metallic bands that formed her mouth fell open. She gently stroked his fuzzy cheek.

"Kaizon, why?" Blossom said in a shallow whisper. "Why did you protect me? I would have survived the shot, but you ..."

She pressed her lips together, then slowly ran her fingers down his eyelids, closing them forever. Her voice shifted timber, becoming rough and growly in the language of the Krurgik, which Croft's earpiece translated.

"Through the Umbec Waters I descend to join Ysarra in the Holy Depths. Peaceful be my slumber until Tegaran calls me again. Until then, farewell."

Croft blinked away tears, which floated mercilessly before him. His chest felt as if the entire weight of *Majestic* sat squarely upon it.

Eckle had just murdered a good man simply to make a point.

Maria covered her mouth, her brown eyes fixed on the floating red corpse. A thin whine escaped through her fingers. Eckle had called her bluff, and Kaizon had paid the price.

Another whine built beside Croft, but this one lowered in pitch until its rage vibrated his ears like a war drum. The electric arcs in Blossom's eyes flared with Zeus's fury, crackling like twin thunderstorms. Her whine became a yell, then a scream. She turned on Eckle, the fingers of her one hand curled into talons.

"You took him from me! *You took him from me!*"

If Eckle was intimidated by the show that would have made Croft quake in his space suit, armored or no, he gave no indication. With a lazy sigh, he swung his rifle in the direction of her main processor.

Blossom grabbed her umbilical cable and whipped it in a circular motion. At the same time, she kicked off the wall so hard that her toes left deep scores in the metal, launching herself at ballistic speed on a collision course with Eckle.

Eckle had just lined up his aim when the whip-like cable arced up and wrapped around his weapon. The rifle fired off-angle, scorching the ground, but nothing else.

By the time he realized what had happened, Blossom was on him. She grabbed his weapon with her one remaining arm, then spun her feet toward him and kicked his chest like a raging rodeo bull. Eckle flew backward and crashed against the far wall. He quickly regained his senses and aimed his rifle once again to fire.

Except his hands were empty. Blossom held his rifle in her trembling grip.

"You took him from me," she said, quiet as death.

She slowly raised the rifle. Its glowing barrel pointed straight at Eckle's head.

"A life for a life." She gripped the handle so hard that it creaked. "By Rragur's Justice, your life is mine!"

Croft held his breath. He couldn't stand the idea of a gentle person like Blossom taking another life, but neither could he begrudge her right to do so.

Her finger closed on the trigger. Eckle put his arms in front of his face and cringed.

A second passed. Then two. Then ten.

Nothing happened.

Blossom growled, throaty and electric. Her hand shook with visible effort. Her finger hovered over the trigger, but wouldn't move the final centimeter necessary to finish the job.

And Croft suddenly realized why.

Her directives!

Blossom was a racing pilot, not a fighter pilot. Killing not only went against her nature, her core programming likely forbade it. She couldn't kill Eckle if he were about to murder a crowd of children.

Eckle's smile indicated he'd just realized it, too.

Croft launched from the wall at the same time as Eckle. Unfortunately, the yellow bird man was closer to Blossom than Croft. If he wrestled that rifle away —

"Blossom!" Maria said, waving her hands. "Throw it here! *Here!*"

Now why didn't I think of that?

Probably because of the ten gallons of adrenaline running through me, he answered himself.

Croft's mind and jittery body wanted to act — which was good, because he couldn't change his collision course with Eckle and Blossom.

Eckle closed fast. His hands stretched for the weapon, still pointed at him by Blossom.

Just when Croft thought he would succeed, Blossom flung it sideways. Eckle spun and groped after it. His fingers missed by a hair's width, but it was enough. The rifle sped safely out of his reach on a trajectory for Maria.

He crashed into Blossom shoulder-first. She wasted no time, grabbed her umbilical cable, and wrapped it twice around his torso, pinning his arms to his sides. Eckle screeched something that didn't translate. He writhed and fought to free himself, but Blossom wound the cable around her wrist, planted her knee against his back, and pulled with all her might to keep the cable tight.

"Croft, do something! I don't know how long I can hold him!"

Fortunately, Croft knew *exactly* how to help.

The pair rotated toward him just as he neared. Croft cocked his arm and, as he'd been itching to do since they'd met, walloped the bug-eyed birdman full in his smarmy face.

His fist caught Eckle partially in the beak. Pain exploded across two knuckles, making Croft see stars. Eckle and Blossom pitched into a backward spin with the blow. Croft bounced off the nearest wall and launched himself again. When he neared, he kicked down on Eckle's legs to stop their spin, then caught Eckle with a left punch, aiming beside his beak this time to avoid breaking any more fingers. The birdman's head snapped back. His beady eyes unfocused.

On the next revolution, his eyes had closed, his body relaxed in unconsciousness.

• • •

Croft tied the final knot, binding Eckle's hands behind his back and to the wires around his ankles, securing him prison-style. Blossom watched, but didn't see. Her eyes slid beyond their captive, in the opposite direction of the corpse behind her that she had been studiously ignoring.

He set Eckle adrift and floated closer to the grieving robot. "Blossom —"

"I don't want to talk." The electric arcs in her eyes had faded to near invisibility. "You and Maria should go."

His heart froze. "You're ... not coming with us?"

Blossom shook her head. "My real body is here — dead — along with Kaizon. It's where I belong. Please, just leave me be."

Damnit, Croft thought, grounding his teeth.

In attempting to save her, they'd accelerated Blossom's self-destructive path to what appeared to be the point of no return. The woeful irony made him want to scream.

"Croft," Maria said from the other side of the hangar, where Kaizon's body floated. "Croft! Blossom! I-I feel a pulse!"

Blossom's metal feet stuck to the floor and had clanked halfway across the room before Croft could even orient himself to kick off from a nearby railing. By the time he made it over to them, Blossom had Kaizon cradled in her lap, her hands stroking either side of his head. She leaned over and gazed intently at his face.

"Kaizon? Can you hear me? Please say something!"

He remained still. To Croft, he didn't appear to be breathing, but then he was hardly an expert on krurgik physiology.

Maria put a hand on her shoulder. "He needs medical attention. *Majestic* has a Type 2 Autodoc on board. It isn't a match for a full medical suite, but it might keep him alive until we get him back to the Truck Stop."

"Well w-what are we waiting for? Let's get him inside! *Hurry!*"

Blossom grabbed him and kicked off on a direct course for *Majestic's* open airlock. She made it ten meters before her umbilical cable yanked tight, jerking her to a halt. She screamed loud, long, and shrill, pulling at her own lifeline as if it were a shackle chaining her to Hell.

"Blossom, don't!"

Croft kicked off to meet her, where Maria joined them. He gently restrained the flailing robot to keep her from hurting herself.

"Don't," he said softly into her audio receiver. "Maria is a trained Autodoc operator. She'll make sure he's hooked up properly and prepare the ship for departure."

"No, I'll take him! Kaizon needs me! Unhook me! *Unhook me!*"

Seeing that she was beyond reason, Croft nodded to Maria and gently restrained Blossom. Maria pulled Kaizon from Blossom's one-armed grip, which elicited more screams. Then, with a push from Croft, she made it to the ship and disappeared inside.

While Blossom flailed and struggled to reach *Majestic,* Croft pulled them along her umbilical cable back to her main processing unit. Miraculously, the double-clamped electrical wires had held throughout the entire harried ordeal.

"Blossom," he said amid her screaming, "I need you to shut down. I'm going to disconnect your power so we can take you with us on *Majestic.*"

"No! Kaizon needs me! *He needs me!*" She struggled in his arms, as she had the entire time, trying to claw her way back to the ship.

With a heavy heart, Croft unclamped one of the power wires from her processing unit.

Blossom's frantic yells abruptly quieted. Her body went limp in his arms.

Croft pressed his forehead to her shoulder, tears welling. He hadn't wanted to be so draconian, but she'd left him no other choice. He looked back at *Majestic,* whose engines were just roaring to life.

Heaven help her if Kaizon doesn't make it.

To his surprise, Maria joined him shortly after. He arched an eyebrow and glanced back to where her patient awaited.

"He's stable," Maria said. "I didn't think the Autodoc would be able to handle him, but apparently krurgik physiology is a standard data set. Eckle's energy shot cauterized Kaizon's wound and stopped the bleeding, which is probably the only reason he's alive. He still needs proper medical attention, but it's looking positive." She hugged herself and glanced at Blossom's limp form. "Need a hand?"

"More than a hand." Croft gestured at the Rhazarian console Blossom had used. "I'm not convinced the smash grid won't reactivate before we return, which might diminish our salvage claim. Besides, I'd like to see if there's anyway to use this facility to repair Blossom, or at least get started. Would you mind poking around to see what you can find?"

Maria blew a long sigh. "Alien languages were never my strong suit, but I'll see what I can do."

"Thanks."

On a whim, Croft kissed her cheek. Maria blinked in surprise. Her full lips broke into a smile, which grew during her brief flight to the console.

A few loose ends tightened and a strap around her umbilical cable secured Blossom for transport. Before taking her back to the ship, Croft floated over to Maria.

"How's progress?"

"Slow," Maria said, glancing between her data pad and the console. "How did you disable the defenses the first time?"

"Blossom."

"Ah. That's a problem, then." She returned her focus to the screen, brows furrowed in concentration.

"Want some help?"

"I'd love it."

The two of them worked together for the better part of an hour, shoulder to shoulder, talking, testing, and trying to make sense of the alien interface. Despite the dire circumstances, Croft found it nice to be working together with her on a common project, instead of the two of them doing their own things, like they usually did.

Maria eventually sighed and ran her fingers through her long hair. "Are you sure this is the right console?"

"Positive. It's in here somewhere."

"Fine. What about this symbol? The translator says 'bearing,' which sounds off, but it's one of the few we haven't tried."

Croft shrugged and tapped the symbol.

A map of the base appeared, along with a red dot to indicate their current position.

Maria squinted at it. "Wait, that can't be right." She used two fingers to zoom in. The room they occupied was as large as Croft's entire workbay at home, yet it represented just a small fraction of the base.

"What is this place?"

"I don't know." Croft began scrolling around. More hangars of equal size or larger ringed the asteroid, and in the center …

"Holy Mother Universe," Croft said softly, an inkling of realization slowly dawning on him.

He floated to the back wall and located what he'd hoped to find: a seam running almost the entire width of the room. He traced it to one end and found what appeared to be a button. Trembling with anticipation, he pushed it.

Metal groaned where the ship had impacted, but slowly a large section of the wall lifted up.

The spectacle beyond stole his breath.

The asteroid was hollow. Inside the vast space sat a staggering array of scaffolds, robotic arms, and equipment, along with two partially constructed star ships, each many times larger than *Majestic* and the Cheybok combined.

Croft turned to Maria. His mouth fell open, but a well of incredulous excitement made it impossible to speak.

This wasn't just a repair base. It was an entire Rhazarian production shipyard.

Maria stared at the complex facility and slowly shook her head. "W-what does this mean?"

So many things, Croft thought, his lips quivering.

"It … it means I'm going to need a partner," he said. "Someone with enough business sense to operate a shipyard."

Maria gasped. "Croft! Do you have the faintest idea how hard it is to run a shipyard? The supply logistics alone are insane! Then you have a small colony of laborers, balancing material costs, electronics, quality assurance, security, licensing and inspection from dozens of interstellar species, and a million other things I'm probably forgetting! Although …" She tapped her lip. "I *do* have an uncle who used to supervise a Martian shipyard. He may be able to give us some pointers."

Croft grinned. He recognized that gleam in her eye. The idea of a new enterprise intrigued her, and he could tell from her wrinkled brow that her mind was already churning over the possibilities. With Maria, it was never *if,* but *how,* a trait he loved about her now more than ever.

At the risk of derailing her thoughts, Croft took her hand, recapturing her attention.

"Maria," he said, his mouth suddenly dry, "will you be my partner?"

She frowned. "Of course. I thought that was a given."

"N-no, not that kind of partner."

Croft reached into his pocket and produced the crystal ring he'd found earlier, lowered himself to one knee, and flashed a nervous, hopeful smile.

EPILOGUE

EIGHTEEN MONTHS LATER

B LOSSOM SHOT ACROSS Croft's workspace like a crossbow bolt, performed a mid-air somersault, ricocheted off the far wall, then caught herself on the chair next to him.

"Come on, it's almost time!" She tugged his arm, bouncing like a kid at her birthday party. "Come on, come *on!* Everyone's waiting!"

"All right!" Croft said, laughing.

He tugged the cuffs of his black tuxedo jacket. Formal wear was Maria's thing, not his, but this was a special occasion. He wouldn't ruin it for Maria by being stubborn about his wardrobe.

"Aren't you dressing up?"

"Nah." Blossom swept her hands up and down her polished, silver-and-purple metallic body. "I'm pretty enough as-is."

"Is that so?" Croft flashed a teasing grin. "Did Kaizon tell you that?"

"As a matter of fact, he did! Last night over dinner. I think he likes me being free of my umbilical cable even more than I do."

"Well, you can both thank the Rhazarians for that."

Installing her processors *and* an independent power reactor inside her small frame had been a daunting prospect at first, but the Rhazarian shipyard had proven to be more than just that. Facilities existed to create every aspect of a ship, including power, electronics, and artificial crew. Utilizing the base's advanced design software, manufacturing a new body for her with similar aesthetics had been a solar breeze.

And she seems to love it.

"How's Maria doing?"

Blossom rolled her arcing electric eyes. "*Waiting,* like everyone else. Now come on before they start without us!"

"Like they would ever start without *you,*" Croft said, letting himself be pulled along.

"You never know. Humans are quirky and a little impatient."

Says the kettle to the pot, Croft thought, suppressing a grin.

Outside, Croft had never seen a larger crowd, and especially not here. Faces familiar and new filled the Rhazarian hangar, talking excitedly in their best attire. Serving bots circulated sealed champagne tubes, *hors d'oeuvres,* and anything else that struck their guests' fancies. Kaizon had pulled out all the stops, for once, and insisted this be an occasion everyone would remember. Also a first, Maria had agreed. She'd even opened their coffers to truly celebrate.

Organic and artificial lifeforms greeted him on his way through the crowd. Croft stopped by a trio of familiar bots and clamped a hand on one's shoulder.

"Quaxlig, glad you could make it."

"The honor is mine, Mr. Winder." The surgical bot dipped its domed head in deference. "Thank you very much for inviting me."

"And me," Taft said. "I did not believe we would be allowed to attend, but Mr. Winder must have presented a very convincing argument." It swiveled to Blossom. "Congratulations. You must be very happy."

"Thanks, I am!"

"Will we be able to see it soon?"

"Very! Speaking of ..." Blossom looked at the nearly identical robot standing next to Taft. "Bult, are you ready? It's almost time!"

The squat robot teetered as if it might fall over, despite the lack of gravity. "Perhaps someone else would be a better choice ..."

"Nope! Too late for that. We've got to get to the podium now." She tugged one of the bot's many arms, along with Croft's sleeve, and nodded to the others. "Have fun, and thanks for coming!"

Taft and Quaxlig waved their spindly arms at their departure.

They met Maria and Kaizon at the top of a podium in the middle of the large hangar.

Maria frowned at Croft's approach. "You're late. Again."

"Sorry. Perfection takes time, and I wanted to look my best."

"*Touché.*" She smoothed his lapel. Her crystal ring sparkled almost as brightly as her eyes. "You do look nice, Mr. Winder."

"Why thank you, Mrs. Winder. So do you."

They shared a blissful smile, interrupted only by Blossom's impatient *ahem.*

"Save the mushy stuff for later. On with the show!"

"Do as she asks," Kaizon said, crossing his arms, "or you'll never hear the end of it. Trust me."

"All right, then."

Croft opened a comm channel on his data pad to the crew inside. He started to speak, but Blossom snatched it from his grip and put it to her eager metallic lips.

"Bring her out! Careful, now. One scratch and you'll be cleaning space dust from the *outside* of the base for a week!"

Maria leaned close to Croft and whispered into his ear. "Funny how a little authority changes some people, isn't it?"

"Oh, I'm sure she's just excited."

"Mm."

Thunder rang through the hangar when the rear doors began to open. Blossom tossed Croft's forgotten data pad, which spun up toward the ceiling, and clutched Kaizon's arm so tightly that he grunted. Her rapt gaze fixed on the opening doors.

The ship's round nose appeared first, capped by an advanced thruster, then the rest of its sleek body followed. The new racer glided into the main hangar with a panther's grace.

Blossom clapped her hands and squealed over the crowd's collective *awwww.* The instant the ship stopped in front of them, she grabbed the bottle of champagne from under the podium and handed it to Bult.

"It's all you! Do your thing so we can actually *fly!*"

Bult teetered again at the edge of the stairs, but accepted the bottle with a nod, along with the microphone. It disengaged its foot magnets and kicked off at a precise trajectory toward the bow, where it swiveled and reattached to the ship. It raised the microphone and started to speak, then seemed to think better of it, yanked the wireless module out of the bottom, and plugged it directly into a port in its chest.

"I would firstly like to thank Ms. Blossom, Mr. Terazod, and Mr. and Mrs. Winder for granting me this unprecedented honor," Bult said with crystal clarity. "Of the many esteemed scholars and businesspersons present, granting a mere luggage robot the opportunity to speak on this auspicious occasion says more about your good character than any amount of fancy *hors d'oeuvres* could."

The applause wasn't as loud as Croft would have liked, but better than he expected.

Baby steps.

"Second," Bult said, "I would be remiss if I did not congratulate the Winders on their recent marriage."

Huge cheers this time. Guilt heated Croft's neck, but he nodded thanks all the same. He kissed Maria's cheek, who beamed with the same pride she had on their wedding day.

"And lastly," Bult said, "for the reason we are all gathered. Eighteen months of concerted effort across scientists, governments, and private investment have culminated in the grand opening of Winder Shipyard, and the christening of its first production ship. Not only is this the first Rhazarian vessel to have graced our galaxy in untold years, it is uniquely owned by its embedded autopilot, Blossom.

"I am aware that this motion is unpopular, but I can only hope that her shining example encourages more such acts, creating a kinder future for biological and artificial lifeforms alike.

"Also, while the Rhazarian's method of inter-galactic travel remains a mystery, by combining our collective knowledge and resources, I am confident that we will one day soon journey beyond the confines of our galaxy and greet the lifeforms we meet as equals.

"And so, without further ceremony, I christen this ship the *Blossom II!*"

The champagne bottle shattered against the bow. People cheered.

Blossom squealed and launched herself with open arms toward the ship, where her brand-new life awaited.

ABOUT THE AUTHOR

Ryan Southwick wanted to be the next Douglas Adams. He isn't, but he hopes you enjoyed this book anyway.

Find out more by visiting *ryansouthwickauthor.com*.

ALSO IN THIS SERIES

THE STARGAZER GIFT SHOP

by Steve Soult

What would you buy at the Stargazer Gift Shop at the center of the galaxy?

COKE MACHINE

by Vanessa MacLaren-Wray

Every truck stop needs a coke machine.

BETTER ANGELS

by Steven D. Brewer

After trailing a notorious trafficker across the galaxy, a self-appointed guardian angel arrives at the Truck Stop.

THE SMUGGLERS

by Vanessa MacLaren-Wray

Attachment is everything.

Available from Water Dragon Publishing in
hardcover, trade paperback, digital, and audio editions
waterdragonpublishing.com

ALSO BY THE AUTHOR

ANGELS IN THE MIST

THE Z-TECH CHRONICLES BOOK ONE

An ancient, powerful evil is loose in San Francisco. The heart of Silicon Valley must fight back the only way they know how — with compassion, unwavering determination, and, of course, super-technology.

ANGELS LOST

THE Z-TECH CHRONICLES BOOK TWO

A vampire hunter has his sights on Anne Perrin, threatening to unleash the very evil she and her friends are fighting to contain.

ANGELS FALL

THE Z-TECH CHRONICLES BOOK THREE

Charlie's life force is fading. His only hope is an aged martial arts master in the remote reaches of China who, as far as Cappa can tell, doesn't like him very much.

ANGELS FOUND

THE Z-TECH CHRONICLES BOOK FOUR

An ancient evil in Anne's head aims to ruin her tranquil life and end humanity. It must be Tuesday.

ZIMA: ORIGINS

A Z-TECH CHRONICLES STORY

Even artificially intelligent recovering assassins need a home.

ONCE UPON A NIGHTWALKER

A Z-TECH CHRONICLES STORY

Ellen Bloom just wants a normal working relationship with her colleagues at her old job. But, at this point, she'd be happy with a pulse.

Available from Water Dragon Publishing in
hardcover, trade paperback, digital, and audio editions
waterdragonpublishing.com